Self Portraits: Fictions

ALSO BY FREDERIC TUTEN

The Green Hour

Van Gogh's Bad Café

Tintin in the New World

Tallien: A Brief Romance

The Adventures of Mao on the Long March

Self Portraits: Fictions

Frederic Tuten

W. W. NORTON & COMPANY
New York • London

Copyright © 2010 by Frederic Tuten

For information about permission to reproduce
selections from this book, write to Permissions,
W. W. Norton & Company, Inc.,
500 Fifth Avenue, New York, NY 10110

For information about special discounts for bulk
purchases, please contact W. W. Norton Special Sales
at specialsales@wwnorton.com or 800-233-4830

Manufacturing by Courier Westford
Book design by Chris Welch
Production manager: Anna Oler

Library of Congress Cataloging-in-Publication Data

Tuten, Frederic.
Self portraits : fictions / Frederic Tuten. — 1st ed.
p. cm.
ISBN 978-0-393-07905-0 (hardcover)
I. Title.
PS3570.U78S45 2010
813'.54—dc22

                                  2010019761

W. W. Norton & Company, Inc.
500 Fifth Avenue, New York, N.Y. 10110
www.wwnorton.com

W. W. Norton & Company Ltd.
Castle House, 75/76 Wells Street, London W1T 3QT

1 2 3 4 5 6 7 8 9 0

For Alain Resnais,
mon cher ami,
with admiration and love

"What do you want for your fifth birthday?"

"Either a microscope or a telescope."

"What do you want with a microscope?"

"To see small things."

"And a telescope?"

"To see the man in the moon."

"Is there a man in the moon?"

"No. But I want to see him anyway."

Contents

Self Portraits: Fictions

Prologue

She was a thin woman without much fantasy. In her dress, I mean. Black from head to toe, in the Sicilian manner. She was a Sicilian, in fact, and she was my grandmother. She spoke little and, to my humiliation—I wanted to be like the other American kids in the Bronx—in Sicilian. And then, too, we were at the tail end of the war with Italy. So that in the street and other public places, I answered her in English to distance myself.

Not that my Sicilian was great. But at eight or nine I managed to tell her what she wanted to know about my world at school and to conduct her from butcher to grocer and order for her and to check the scales when she thought they were tipping high. Unless we walked some distance to Arthur Avenue, where she did not require my help, because you could—and probably still can—spend your whole life there speaking only Italian. But then, we would have had to spend the nickel bus fare to carry back the shopping all that distance home, so we mostly stayed in the neighborhood and I watched the scales. She also thought, in the Sicilian fashion, never to ask directions of a policeman because it was not wise to approach the law for whatever reason. Just out of perversity, because we were greenhorns, he might point us the wrong way.

I also, and more importantly, served as her translator for the American news on the radio, and for the American movies. There were plenty of Italian-American programs on the radio, especially the soap operas she loved, but she did not trust the news as reported in her language, because she believed the wartime censorship was greater for the Italian audience.

The movies were where I shined best, interpreting for her most of the dialogue she missed, which was most of the dialogue. Sometimes I myself didn't understand what was happening on the screen, the love scenes especially, when suddenly the couple stopped speaking, while the music rose and the camera cut away to a train going through a tunnel or to a horse rearing in its stable.

"*Che cosa successo?*" What's happening? she'd ask me in a whisper too loud for those about us. Or in English: "What he say?" More humiliation for me. But at least it was suffered in the dark.

At those times when I lost the film's thread, I invented the story just to keep her happy, hoping she would not notice the discrepancy between the action on the screen and my childish interpretation. "He's tired and he wants to go to sleep," I explained, as the lead walked into his girlfriend's bedroom.

My mother was the firstborn in America, and while she could read and write, she had to help support the family and left high school at fifteen and she went to work in Manhattan's garment center. My grandfather never learned to speak English. He died longing for Sicily, where he could speak his language everywhere, even in the streets. My mother was raised in an all-Italian-speaking household. And, except when my father—whose family was in America before the Revolution—on the increasingly rare occasion came home, I was, too.

My mother read romances alone in the bedroom, and I read in the living room I shared with my grandmother—a screen separating the two cots across the room. My mother never told us about the novels she was reading, going to her bed, book in hand, exhausted after dinner and after a long day at work as a draper more than an hour and a half away in Manhattan. I was fascinated by what she was reading, by what kept her so absorbed as to keep her from me.

Romances were her special fare: pirate and historical novels with sizzling jackets, books she rented for pennies a day from the stationery store near her subway station. Books I was yearning to read and one day would. But for the moment, in that living room or at the kitchen table, I was buried in my own books of the faraway: R. L. Stevenson's *Kidnapped*, *Ali Baba and the Forty Thieves*; *Tom Sawyer*; The *Hardy Boys* series; picture books of exotic travel into deserts and jungles; and maybe, when I was ten, H. Rider Haggard's *She*, a travel-adventure with its mysterious story of a beautiful woman who stayed young a thousand years to wait for her lover to return.

My grandmother did not read. She claimed she could not see the print because of cataracts, which in those days and at her old age were difficult to remove. But I suspect she was illiterate, never having gone to school in Sicily, where she was married at fifteen and where she bore four children, two of whom died of measles. I read for her. Not in the conventional way of translating word-for-word my childhood books, but by telling her—with my own editing and inventions—the stories in my reading.

From me she learned how an American boy and a slave fled home on a raft on a river a thousand times bigger than the Bronx River running through the Botanical Garden not far away from us, and how a man discovered the secret word for opening a cave in Arabia where outlaws hid their "loot"—I used the English word for that—of gold and jewelry in huge barrels, like the ones heaping with olives and dried sardines in the markets of Arthur Avenue. I was a great storyteller, she said, which emboldened me to further inventions and recon-structions of these children's classics. My only rivals for her entertainment, I believe, were her radio soaps and the mov-ies—where I also wielded some narrative power.

I knew one storytelling device which always worked. I would reach a crucial point in my tale—such as, "He was in the outlaws' cave bathing himself in gold coins, when he heard a loud noise behind him"—and then I would pause.

"*E poi?*" And then? she would invariably ask.

The same "and then" that is the fulcrum of all fiction, going back to the earliest time our ancestors sat about the communal fire spellbound by tales; the "and then" that moves the narrative forward and, most of all, keeps the reader or the listener hooked on yearning to know more of the story.

"And then, Grandma," I said, "he turned and saw the heavy cave door shut behind him."

That narrative device, that pause and withholding of information, I had learned from her when she told me her own stories, no less wonderful to me than the ones I had been reading and reinventing.

Her husband had been a policeman, one of the few carabiniere in her village, where they had a home and a small vineyard in the hills. Rich grapes to make golden muscatel.

"*E poi?*" I asked.

He went after some bandits in the mountains. They had been robbing people in the village. The bandits sent word to leave them alone or they would hurt his family. He went after them still. That was his stubborn way.

"*E poi?*"

They burned the vineyard and they said they would burn the house next, and then they would kill the children.

"*E poi*, Grandma?"

"Then they burned the house. And then we left for America."

We sat, we two, in the Bronx, telling stories in a darkish room, safely away from the frightening world outside the window, where the police gave misdirections and the butcher tipped the scale.

Stories. Like air, like food, like hope. I read them, I told them, and later, I wrote them, stories about men and women seeking the faraway in revolutions, in art, and in the dreamy search for love, but by that time she, Francesca, my first muse, was gone.

Voyagers

Enriching, travel was. Deepening my conviction that there was little to live for, little reason to live, less to be born. I thought I would tell her that before we finished our dinner and left separately for the night.

A black gondola, minus the oarsman, was skimming toward her; some inches away, separated by blue molding, Vesuvius showered smoke and flaming embers over her head. She seemed in a low mood, but I had thought that of her many times before and was often shown wrong. She was sometimes just in no mood for me, for my accustomed face. I did not blame her. So large a world, so many fresh faces to consider.

"Listen," she said.

I had traversed many deserts and arid places: the Empty Quadrant, the Sahara, the Gobi, the Mojave, the Sands of

Dreams, the Wastes of Longing. On various crafts I had plied many rivers, as well: the Mississippi, the Amazon, the Tocantins, the Yangtze, the Orinoco, the Nile, the Río de Alegría, the River of Disappointments, the River of Sorrows.

Having had, long ago, a vision—at once ravishing and disappointing in its inconclusivity—a vision on a cliff, I came to avoid all mountains, hills, and high places, all heights above three ladder steps, conducting my life at elevations well beneath the clouds. Caves, canyons, arroyos, valleys, trenches, cellars, basements, subways, tunnels, all man-made declivities below sea level I also shunned. What is there waiting beneath the surface of the earth but the grave?

The lugubrious waiter, with the quick hand of a pickpocket, had long ago lifted away her plate. Mine, too. And now she pushed aside her empty wineglass, suggesting that all impediments had finally been vanquished, and that nothing but space and time stood between us. Her clavicle rose where her blouse was spread open two buttons below her still creamy neck. Her lips parted.

"Listen," she said.

Once: A small campfire, blue flames biting the night. Pebbles glowing dully in the blackest sky. The two tethered camels dozed, lapsing into camel dreams. I slept wrapped in a blue wool blanket, on a Berber carpet, the cold so cold. My Beretta in hand, the safety off. Desert lions in the hills, bandits in the dunes. The man—my guide—on watch had often proven unreliable, dozing away with the camels, so I slept fitfully, waking every now and then to gape at the reassuring stars and to glance over to his post. I heard a scuffle just before dawn and woke to find Ali upright and smiling at me with two smiles. His rifle was gone and the water bags and his father's gold ring, as well as the little finger it had encircled.

They left me to make my way out of the desert alone, knowing they could pick me off sooner or later, whenever they wished. Left me to wander about without water and without hope, until they plucked me from the delirious sands. It would be more pleasurable for them to kill me that way than to cut my throat outright on the spot, along with Ali that night.

On the fifth day of wandering, I slit my camel's underside and drank his oozing blood, and with my blood-dipped finger wrote on the leather saddlebag the name Marie.

"Are you listening?" she said.

Once: Long ago, she stood by the lion cage in the Bronx Zoo. Hand in hand with her mother. Red jacket, square Prussian blue buttons, shiny black shoes, black leggings, hair in black bow, white suede gloves. I detached myself from my father and ran up to her and kissed her cheek. A sleepy old lion yawned a giant yawn, devouring up half the stars in the world. I took her hand, drawing her back from the cage and the lion's great groan, back from the lion himself and his threatening appetites.

"Marie," I whispered in her ear. "Marie, let's run far away."

"To the elephants and the seals?" she asked.

No, not to them. Not to the camels and their haughty

indifference. Not to the chimps, who would belittle our love with their lewd antics. Not to the donkey cart, to ride hand in hand in circles under the shady trees only to end up where we had begun. No, I would take her on my silvery pirate ship and sail away to the palm trees and the icebergs, sail until we grew ancient and our weary vessel sank in a milky green bay bordered by golden sands.

She turned to look for the waiter. Then she turned another way to look for the waiter. The gondola advanced toward her; the volcano's raining embers more closely threatened her head.

Once: All manner of hell broke loose on the Irish Sea. Gale force 9. The steel rigging snapped and went whipping about the deck and smacked the mate into the roiling swells. In the thick of a BBC chat on how to care for roses in sudden frosts or after great deluges of rain, the radio died midsentence. Then the sea anchor tore from its rode, sending our trawler spinning in the churning night. Finally, when the rudder snapped, the captain took us in his confidence.

"Well, boys," he said. "It's each man for himself."

I promptly took his advice and raced belowdecks and drew out her last letter from the packet stashed in my footlocker. Shaky reading, that, with the overhead lights blinking on and off and off and on, with all that rolling and lolling and tossing and bucking. Then we went down, me and the letter and the ship, just as I was reading her closing line. *Don't*, it began, as we plunged bows on into the deep.

"Are you listening?" she asked.

It was unusually quiet in the room and in the ones below and above. The streets silent, the skies silent, the clouds rumbled silently in their drift. Clickety clackity my typewriter from time to time, when I pecked at it with three fingers, to disturb the silence. Then, out from the quiet, a faraway zap and maybe a cry or maybe a crash of glass. I drew the heavy velvet curtain across the windows and moved my chair and little desk to the center of the room, directly under the crystal chandelier and opposite the painting of a shepherdess feeding a cluster of pink grapes to a bearded satyr.

Marie, I wrote, beginning a new sentence.

The phone rang and continued its ringing until I finally decided to answer. I was to leave the room and take the stairs directly to the basement. "Please do not stop at the bar, sir," the man at the other end of the connection said, politely, I thought. A few of us were known to sit at the bar when the shelling began, and to remain there as long as the shelling continued and even after the lights blew out.

"Don't worry," I told the bartender one day. "We're keeping track of the liquor bill."

That was frivolous of me, a kind of showing off—bravado stuff. She would have despised me a full month had she heard me bluster so.

I went down, bypassing the bar entirely as requested, and joined the twenty others all sitting quietly in a row on ballroom chairs. After a while the ceiling shook. The lights went out but we weren't worried about the lights, only about the ever-nearing giant thuds and the shrieking of cracking beams and splintering glass. We didn't have to worry about the lights going out because the basement was glowing with oil lamps and small candles borrowed from the dinner tables above. But some, who carried flashlights, kept checking the ceiling to see if it was threatening to cave in and bury us under plaster and steel.

I tried to plan the rest of the letter so that when I returned to my room I could write it out all in a flash and send it off in the morning and have it behind me. My letter, I mean. She didn't care, she once told me, how long it took a letter to reach her. Nothing electronic, nothing telephonic would do to serve the matters of the heart, only a letter served that organ, and only a letter composed as if it were the last ever to be sent. A letter from the front, so to speak, written in the trenches an hour before the bloody charge at dawn.

I thought to tell her how many bodies I had seen in the streets, and how the old houses and cafés we had known had been gutted by shells and bombs, and how children wandered the hospitals searching for their families among stacks of corpses lining the corridors. Then I thought I would write her about the rooks, hundreds of them perching on the dead trolley wires and crowing for hours without stop, deep cackles and high shrieks and then a kind of chorus of laughter as they watched the bodies being lifted from the rubble and tossed into open trucks. I was still seeing the bodies when the sky fell and lifted me a few inches from my seat and set me down again with my mouth full of plaster and blood. I stayed awhile not moving, and then in the airless dark I began to trace her name on my powdered sleeve.

"I'm leaving for a while," she said.

"Oh!" I said, not very expressively, having, for the moment, no clear idea to express.

"And you? Are you off again?"

"I'm staying put for now," I said.

"Flat tire?"

My tires, including the spare, deflated, I wanted to say, and all the moving parts in arthritic disposition, the motor in collapse; the car itself rusting away in the garage, I would have added, were it necessary.

Eight A.M., 103 F°, the Tocantins River; Sunday, the flat day. Me on deck coiling lines and bending to the will of the sun, shielding myself under a bloodred canopy from its broiling heat. Coffee sacks sweltered in the hold below while we roasted on deck above. The Belgian was casually sobering up at the wheel. He had the shakes and a banging hangover and drank pickle brine straight from the jar to steady himself. "It's the only thing that works," he said, tossing the pickles overboard. He steered a cranky course and sometimes I had to shout out to warn him how close we were to running aground or to ramming a tree trunk half drowned in a flood.

"Typhoons ahead," Willie said from his cage swaying under the canopy.

The parrot was mocking me and the Belgian for the fools we were for steaming down a thousand miles of river to sell coffee and salt and sulfur matches to the little wood and mud shops along the jungle banks. Months of travel, a day's worth of profit.

"Leave it alone, Willie," the Belgian said. He was superstitious and feared all harbingers of disaster.

"Those are pearls that were his eyes," the parrot answered. "'Pearls . . .'"

"I'll come over and wring your shitty neck," the Belgian said, abandoning the tiller long enough for us to list toward a sandbar.

"By god, I'll crack your head if you touch him," I said. "I'll throw you overboard and leave you for the monkeys."

The Belgian raised his fist, but then must have thought the better of it and slinked back to the wheel barely in time to put us back on course.

I sulked the rest of the day and thought to get off at the first village en route and leave the Belgian to fend for himself, but not before I had released Willie to the green world from which he had been abducted as a youth. I went to Willie several times in the course of the day and spoke to him gently, calling him sweet names, and stroked his crown until he puffed and gurgled in parrot joy. In soothing him, I soothed myself, and soon I let myself drift on clouds of unexamined memories, the avenues to nowhere.

At dusk, we moored in a serene inlet, a rush of dark coolness flowing toward us from the jungle. Under a mosquito net, under the stars, each of us, the Belgian and I, without a parting word, he at the bow, me at the stern, bedded down for the night. Soon I drifted to the edge of sleep, an inch from it, when Willie's screech woke me. I opened my eyes to see the Belgian and his hammer crashing down on my head. And just before I went out for the count, as they say, I heard Willie cry out again, but this time crying the name I had taught him to speak in my most lonely moments.

"Marie, Marie," he said, echoing my last words of the night as I sank under the hammer.

"Listen," she said. "You can come visit me whenever you like."

Once, in Tangiers, standing on the cliffs of Old Mountain, at dusk, in that crack of light, we saw God in the weld of sea and sky. Marie was trembling. She turned to me and said, "You're trembling, too." True, but I had not paid attention to it, my trembling, only hers. Thinking, at first, we had been chilled by the wind rising up from the damp sea below, or chilled from the cool breeze of clouds as they floated over us like sluggish dirigibles stuffed with freezing water. Not realizing until we had returned to our hotel room what it had been that caused that trembling. Why had I not thought it natural, when we stood there on the cliffs, up above the world, natural to tremble before God?

We stayed in bed for a long time without speaking. But I finally could not stand the silence.

"Well, Marie," I said. Well, what? I had no idea of what would follow.

"What difference does anything make now?" she said, turning off the table light, leaving the room bathed in silver glow. "No matter what wonderful thing we've seen, we'll soon go back to our old ways," she said.

She was right, of course. It wasn't as if we had been given a commandment or an explanation or a blessing but just a "glimpse of content." And what then would it change, seeing God? I would still travel and she would still travel. We would separate and reunite, as always. The world would spin as always and she and I would drift along with it until the end.

I went up to the open window full of moon and minarets, of palm trees and jasmine, of mint tea and donkeys, of olives in earthen vats, of cinnamon and burnt kef, of sheep slaughtered for God, and I said, in a voice strangely not my own, to the room and to the woman spread out under a sheet drawn just beneath her breasts, I said:

" 'We are floating in a medium of vast extent, always drifting uncertainly, blown to and fro; whenever we think we have a fixed point to which we can cling and make fast, it shifts and leaves us behind.' "

She lifted herself on her elbows and answered in a voice equally as strange as mine, " 'Let us then seek neither assurance nor stability; our reason is always deceived by the inconsistency of appearances; nothing can fix the finite between the two infinities which enclose and evade it.' "

"Visit you where?" I asked.

"Arizona, in the desert someplace. I'd like to garden."

Once she lived alone in Rome, house-sitting a villa with a garden of white roses, then she moved to the Sicilian mountains to live with a shepherd, in a stone cottage his grandfather had built to shelter himself from women. How she had met the shepherd I never knew. His photo profiled a slender young man in trunks, his gaze fixed on the wine-dark sea—a Ulysses without a wife.

"Nothing like the desert," I said, "for gardening."

"Or the Mojave, maybe."

"It's the best for gardening, the desert. The green means so much there in all that dried beige."

She laughed. "Have you turned painter now?"

Once she lived in Paris. Three years. In the working-class suburb of Saint-Denis, in a flat bathed in the mint-green light of a North African café two stories below. With an American bicycle mechanic who read Pascal and Kropotkin. I visited them when they were happy. I wanted to dislike him and hate their happiness, but I admired his unaffected simplicity, his American directness. Then one day they were no longer happy and she left him, without rancor, and with memories of the good years that they had shared. She never spoke ill of him but she never spoke of him again, either. A blip of happiness in the long everyday of life.

"Could that happiness not have been ours?" I one day asked her on a beach in Minorca, the sun killing us under a red umbrella.

"But we have been happy together all our lives," she said.

On reflection, that night, when my trawler was diving down to Davy Jones's Locker, I came to see—in that moment when death seemed just ahead—and to appreciate her point.

Once she lived in Barcelona with a Hungarian artist who painted her dreams, which he asked her to recite to him every morning at breakfast. One day, he painted me naked on a blue horse against chalk cliffs. A giant dirigible raining showers of black ice floated in the distance. After that, I began to show up more and more in the recounting of her dreams, until one day he asked her, "Who is this man who so much lives with you when you are sleeping, lives with you more hours than you spend awake with me?"

"Oh!" she said. "He's the dream."

"And who am I, then?" the Hungarian asked playfully, perhaps expecting her to say he was her living and only reality.

"You are its painter," she answered, without adornment.

Finally, I turned for the waiter and thought I glimpsed a flash of his dark jacket as the door swung open to the kitchen.

"Or you can come and stay with me," she said.

"Well," I said playfully, "are we so close to the journey's end, then?"

She had left the shepherd because he called her a whore for returning a man's glance while they were strolling in the town square one Sunday. She was separated from the Hungarian because when at last he felt his Hungarian charm could not, did not, would never penetrate to the depth of her dreams, he vacated Barcelona and its wonderful parks and more wonderful light, which, in any case, considering he worked wholly in his studio atmosphere, he never had any use for.

"Technically, I'm not leaving you," he said, "because in principle you were never with me to leave."

The restaurant had emptied, though it was well before midnight. A tug sent out a long whistle as it was making its way up or down the East River, the watery road on which I often had begun so many of my voyages.

"Perhaps it's time to come to a rest. Have you ever considered that?" she asked.

Clearly now, our waiter had long vanished along with the plates. Something in his carriage and faraway look had told me from the start, from the moment he plunked down the laminated menus, that he was another fellow of the road, and I guessed that now he had simply walked out the door and had gone down the street to the dark Brooklyn piers and found a passage on a tanker or a freighter bound for Peru. Indeed, no tip was worth staying for. I myself many times in the past had shipped out from those nearby docks and I had, on vessels of various sizes, crossed the oceans and several seas. The Red, the Yellow, the Arabian, the Indian, the Mediterranean, the Ionian, the Caspian, the Sargasso, the Sea of Hope, the Sea of Forgetfulness, and the yet vaster Sea of Desire.

I was a proven friend of the watery world, gulfs were ponds to skip across. I could easily have boarded the gondola overhead and sculled over the Venetian lagoons and pushed out to the open Adriatic, whose ashen waters I strangely had never plied. But I was now imagining a berth for a longer, more novel voyage out, ships large and small filling quickly day and night, packed to the gills and stacked high to the gunnels, but always with room for more. Room, at the very least, for one more.

Self Portrait with Sicily

"Have you been away a long time?" the short Sicilian asked, looking away from me.

"Is it my accent that makes you ask? Do I sound foreign?" I added. I was alarmed to think that I had changed so obviously over the years. He did not answer but went on hungrily eating hunks of bread he tore from a brown paper bag.

The train turned, mountains on one side, the cranky sea on the other. Lemon and orange trees, fields of wild rosemary, crowded the sky and invaded my memories.

We were moving so slowly that I could see my grandmother through our kitchen window as she was spooning snails into a boiling kettle. "Pull down the shade," I called out, wanting no one to see that we ate snails, because when I was a boy no Americans my age ate them—worms with oily shells. Nor did they eat the dandelion leaves my grandmother—a black silhouette—plucked from the Bronx Park fields, just some few miles from the outskirts of Palermo, where streetlamps spread rectangle shrouds on the winter-night streets.

"You people eat grass and worms," the kids cried out when they wanted to start a rock fight with me. Small rocks, hard stones. I still have a scar over my left eye, the one with which I can see the man in the moon and his bucket smile.

She was making the evening meal, my grandmother, and soon we would be at the table putting oil and salt on our bread. And soon we would be eating snails drowned in olive oil and garlic. And then a dandelion salad, bitter like the Bronx winters, the kitchen oven and burners left on all night for the heat. Sometimes there was wine, even for me at ten, from Segesta, where two thousand years ago the Greeks planted temples and sacred groves in whose tranquil shade they turned their minds to reasoning out the world. All that reason wasted in the hills, where hot tempers rule.

"But now you've returned," the short Sicilian said, "now you've come back home."

There were not many automobiles below us in the Bronx streets when I was a boy. It was wartime, the gasoline was rationed; few had cars, and those who did were careful about driving aimlessly here and there just for the carefree joy of taking a spin. In early winter mornings, when I was still half asleep, I could count the handful of autos on the road by the steel rattle of their tires chained against the ice. Everywhere was ice: ice coating the tree branches, ice sheeting the black mountains, ice chilling the little stone houses dotting the frozen hills, ice in my bed piled up with coats for blankets. My grandmother left little chunks of stale bread soaked in muscatel on the windowsill to revive the sparrows freezing in icy winter.

"Poor creatures," she said of them, as they shivered on the windowsill, their beaks blue from the cold.

"I have never left Sicily," I said to the short man, a bit sharply. "Why would you think that?"

Another Sicilian, in a hunter's cap, laughed, as if he had just woken up from a good dream, through whose mist he had found a cave of hidden gold coins as thick as chestnuts. Two gutted hares hung from the staff standing beside him. A double-barrel shotgun rested on his lap like a sleeping child. I liked his green cap, fat and black, and his green hunter's jacket, brushed to a sigh of its used-up life; I liked the way he tried to make himself seem prosperous, though his tired half boots had cords for shoelaces and red patches spiced his dull corduroys.

"Do you have some matches?" he asked, half loading his pipe, his tobacco a peat of leaves and shredded debts.

"Would it not have been polite to ask us whether we minded your smoking in such confined quarters?"

I was gentle in my question, leaving him room to answer me with his dignity intact. You must always leave a man his dignity, unless you hate him. Unless you want to take the chance of his shooting you from behind an orphan tree on a lonely dirt path under the moon stained red by the dying sun and by all the disasters, great and small, that had befallen the day. Stained by the death of a strong goat, say, or of a fierce cat who had kept the rats from bothering the grain, or by an insult that burned and burned in your heart, or by the departure of a hungry son who had gone to work in the factories in the north and who one day would reject all memories of home and who would not even send a threepenny postcard back there.

"I wanted the matches for later," he said. "For when we arrive in Palermo."

"Palermo, is that where you're headed?" I asked the hunter.

"No, why would you think that?" he said, parroting me earlier, when I had asked why he thought I had left Sicily. The other Sicilian laughed, and I did, too, seeing how clever he was, the hunter, as all Sicilians are. Except me, my head filled with books in weary bindings, my head stuffed with dried memories in place of quick thoughts.

The short Sicilian stuffed more bread into his mouth, ballooning his cheeks into a wide pumpkin grin. I was happy for him.

"Are we Sicilians still as hungry as we were fifty years ago?" I asked the bread eater, asking all of Sicily, where, when I was a child, some had much and even more than much to eat and others sipped bowls of warmed water for their dinner.

"Because you are fed, do you think the world is fed?" he replied, licking the little shreds of bread stuck between his teeth.

"We Sicilians are always hungry," the hunter said. "It is in our nature to be hungry, food or no food."

"Is that why we eat sparrows?" I asked.

"To consume sparrows is in our nature," said the hunter.

"To eat baked sparrows is much in our nature," the short Sicilian said. "To eat even their crusty beaks."

"In my region, we do not eat sparrows," I said. "In my region we feed them."

"The region of plenty, I suppose," the bread eater whispered above the grinding of train wheels, whose heedless sparks set fire to towns and villages and wooden shacks along the way.

"The region of pity," I said, "is where we lived, the region of pity." That remark seemed to keep them pensive for a while, leaving one to gnaw on his bread and the other on his hunter's dreams.

Now the train was gaining speed, traveling through flaming fields, hot fires the farmers had set to burn the dead stalks of corn, their ash to enrich the depleted soil and return its honor. The train slowed into the station, as empty as an abandoned factory. Tucking the paper bag under his jacket to shelter it from the cascading rain, the short man rose and, with great courtesy, said, "I leave you and I salute you."

"I will miss you," I said. As I would, missing the sparrow

from the windowsill, missing a cloud as it sailed away beyond my view, missing those who had left me even before they had died, missing my life as it sped faster and faster away from me.

Now we were again out of the station and into the countryside, where the sky was sending down a torrent, flooding everywhere lands high and low, engorging the newly planted corn, and drowning everywhere the chickens in their coops and snails in their shells. In Sicily, the sun either burns the earth down to powder or the rain turns it into lakes where families of vipers enjoy their swim on Sundays, when Sicilians at mass pray for a fat roast chicken and potatoes for dinner.

No sooner had the short man left and the train had made its way again, than a young man with a mandolin under his arm entered and, sizing us up for men who did not have the coins to pay for a tune and a song, went into another compartment. Two plainclothes policemen in black silk suits came into our compartment as if they owned it; they looked about, and one, with nails for eyes, gave us stern schoolmasterish looks, as if we had been caught passing smutty notes to each other under our desks.

The hunter doffed his cap to them, to show them he knew his place. I wore no hat but made a little salute and a bow of the head, letting them know that I also knew mine.

"Have you seen here a man with a bag of bread?" the tall one, with grilled-mutton hands, asked.

The hunter and I looked at one another. He shrugged. I shrugged. Then I say, in a respectful voice, "Not me, sir."

Then the other man, the one with nail eyes, said, "I did not hear you speak."

"I saw no such man, Captain," the hunter says, doffing his cap again deferentially.

Then Mutton Hands said, very softly, so as almost not to be heard, so as to make us strain to understand his words, "You're too slow to answer when addressed by significant people."

"It could be taken for an insult," Nail Eyes adds, with a smile to kill a ripe eel.

Then he goes, "What fine hares you have there. Very fat and filled with honey, very ripe for a stew."

"I'm sure," the hunter said with measured dignity, "my wife would be as happy as I knowing that these hares will grace your table tonight."

The men did not smile.

"Your Excellencies," he added, offering them his staff and hares.

The train slowed into the station. "Keep your dinner," Nail Eyes said, "with respects from us to your famous wife, if you find her still at home when you return."

They disembarked, scurrying down the platform, to apprehend one or another poor man who came into their suspicious view.

"They always have an insult to humiliate you or to provoke you into regrettable foolishness," the hunter said. "Why is it always like that?" he asked the hares.

"Power," I said, as if that explained the world. Then I added without thinking, "Sicily."

"But we are in the Bronx," the hunter said.

"It's the same thing," I said.

He studied me for a moment, then asked. "Would you like them?" indicating the hares.

For a moment, I thought of what a fine stew they would make, cooked in red wine, with some carrots for color. But I remembered that I now had no place to cook them, no home and no stove. I thanked him for his offer, saying that I had a long journey ahead and thought it best to make it unencumbered. It was a reasonable excuse and he accepted it with a dignified bow of his head. It seemed that all the police unpleasantness that had threatened to sour our way had been settled and we were now ready to continue our journey along the neutral grounds on which it had begun.

But when the train was some minutes from the station, he rose, lowered the window, and, as we were climbing over the Bronx River, he let fall the staff and dangling hares into the muddy water below. He grinned at me, pleased with his costly triumph, and rubbed his hands on his pants, as if to wipe away the grimy memory of the policeman's insult.

"Well, that's finished," he said, with the finality of a newly dug grave.

There will be other hares, I wanted to assure him, even bigger and ones with more honey than those you have just shot. You are still a young man, after all, I wanted to say. But that was not true. He was not young. But not old, either, having the age of a man who has come to know who he is without falsifications. He must have been fifty, the age, I supposed, when a man has attained wisdom, which, I imagined, would one day also be mine, like a great inheritance, like a ripe vineyard on a hill taller than the rain and clouded from the scorching sun.

Finally, I understood who he was, the hunter, and I said, "Are you not my uncle, Umberto? The one who owned seven mulberry trees and left for America after the Great World War? Are you not the one who gave me five dimes in secret after Sunday mass, a secret between us, lest your son be jealous of your gift to me?"

As we Sicilians are jealous of gifts given to others and worried by the intent of presents given to us, as we Sicilians are worried by everything. A life of worries that not even death has the power to end. We worry in the grave and worry in the few cents' worth of our ashes. I wanted to say all this but thought it unnecessary for the occasion, thinking also that he had known all this, as he was clearly a wise man without falsifications.

"You are that uncle," I continued, "whose quince tree I climbed one day and shook the crows from their strong roost in the clouds."

"You were a good boy, you and that girl, too," he said at last, "saving my quinces from their beaks. Those crows," he said, as if he wished to break their wings and bake them in a pie.

"But they were hungry, those crows," I said, "like most of us in Sicily. Like all of the world who labor and from whose labor others summer in mansions by the sea." My voice trailed off, ashamed at the obviousness of my remarks.

"Your grandmother," he said, changing the subject and gracefully saving me from further embarrassment, "liked to drink a glass of muscatel with a raw egg when she was feeling sick. She was always sick," he said. "She drank the muscatel that I made myself, from my own grapes" he said proudly.

"She was infrequently sick," I said, not liking his speaking of my Nònna in that way, as if she were an invalid. She was, of course, but who wants to review all that? I also did not like that he was so boastful of his insignificant vineyard, the size of a pale sneeze.

The train was coming to the station where my grandmother was to wait for me, and there she was, on the platform, standing exactly at the spot where my door opened. My uncle gave her a polite smile, and she to him. I stepped onto the platform, turning to say goodbye respectfully, and he saluted me. Imagine that, I wanted to say to my grandmother, imagine that I would meet my uncle in a train after not seeing him all these hundreds of years, or so it seems. "But nothing is unusual in Sicily," my grandmother said, reading my thoughts, as she always had, even from miles away.

She took my hand, as she always had when I was a boy,

leading me through the marketplace, barrels and bushels and baskets of snails and olives and salted cod, dirty white like leftover snow, fronting the shops. To my surprise, because it was our usual marketing day, we stopped at none of the stalls but walked out of the district and followed a path through a wood, stands of cypresses flanking our way like blackened arches of a burnt-down church.

"Where are we going?" I asked.

"A surprise," she said.

I became worried that it might be like the surprise she had given me when I was a boy in short pants. One cloudless, burning summer day we took a similar path through similar woods to come upon a smallish Greek temple dedicated to the goddess of plentitude standing in the cypress groves on a cliff above the sea. My grandmother, mixing a bowl of honey and wine for the goddess, ordered me to pray.

Pray, she said, that we can pay the rent, pray that we can pay the electricity to light us through the coming winter. Her offering and our prayers were soon rewarded with a soak-ing rainstorm, the goddess imagining, perhaps, that we were farmers praying for water in a land of drought. My grand-mother was never clear in her prayer, I suppose. Or perhaps over time the goddess had become less Greek and more Sicil-ian, a trickster, granting favors but not the ones prayed for.

"I don't want a surprise, Nònna," I said. "I don't like it here anyway, this is place filled with memories of nothing alive."

I need not have worried because we soon left the temple

and the cypress grove and walked into a field of frozen lava, pocketed here and there with little caves leading down into the underworld of shades.

"There is someone here who has been in my dreams these last three nights, and who has been asking for you," my grandmother said. "It would be disrespectful not to make the visit."

She was right, of course. The dead—lest they sour in their loneliness—must always be visited when they inquire after you.

"Who was in your dreams?" I asked, hoping it was not my mother, whose grave I had failed to visit on the last anniversary of her death. And a few before that, as well, I remembered guiltily.

"No, not she, but another who still thinks of you."

"My wife?" I said, a bit annoyed.

"No, not she, though I'm sure she remembers you all the time, now that the ninny has time for reflection on her life."

My wife had once gone to America to visit her married sister in New York, and when she returned, after only four weeks, she refused to wash the dishes after dinner, saying that she and I should share the job, as the equals that we were. She came back with other such modern ideas, which my grandmother found unnatural to life and demeaning of me, the man of the house, who should never wash the dishes lest he become a woman. I never cared who washed the dishes or who swept the floor, having always done my share of both.

But my grandmother rarely spoke to my wife after she made her declaration of domestic liberation. Grandmothers are even less forgiving than mothers, who themselves also never forgive wrongs done to their sons, I reckoned. The truth is that I never loved my wife, dishes or no dishes. I never loved her in bed, where all life's opera starts and ends. Let's say that she and I were all solos and no duets, no grand soaring to the heavens, no ecstasy. Let's say that one does one's duty when called upon to save one's honor and the honor of the other. But duty does not ignite fires.

"Let it go, *Nònna*," I said. "All that is long ago and no one is pure."

That was true, of course, no one is pure, or half pure, but I wished it were not so, and that we could all live as we did when we were children. But then I recalled how children are mixtures of sweetness and guile, how children can be murderous and jealous, how children are midget versions of ourselves, the grown-ups, who betray with every breath the purity of each clean dawn.

"Yes," I added, "only the olive oil is pure in these days."

"*Figlio mio*," she said, "today the olive oil is often mixed, the good with the inferior."

"Even here in Sicily?" I said.

She tilted her head to give me her knowing look, the one she used to stare down the butcher when he tried to switch rabbit for veal, the look she used to show the world she knew what was what.

We soon came to a declivity, a pocket in the earth the size of a wheelbarrow, from which rose a cold mist that chilled me on the spot. A voice came through the mist or was centered in it, a voice drifting in and out like from an old-fashioned radio with weak reception. I knew that voice. Marie's voice.

How happy I was to hear her! Missing her as I had all these years. Missing her so that nothing else but she filled my bed at night, even when I was not alone in it.

We were in our teen years when we first made love. In the Bronx Botanical Garden, behind some thick bushes ripe with clover and on a bed of daisies and dandelions still moist with spring rain.

"Will you love me forever?" she asked without flourish.

"Yes," I said. As I have, even after she married a school-teacher who had gone to a university, and even after she died at nineteen in childbirth. The child went with her. In Sicily, we die young. The measles, the smallpox, the heartbreak of unrequited love. She had married the wrong man, she con-fessed to me one day, a case of mistaken identity, she said, thinking he was me, just older and more settled in life with a classroom and a pension.

"Marie," I said, "how are you?" It was banal, that, a com-monplace and hollow greeting of the living to the living, but I meant it, wanting to know how she had fared all these years of being dead and what, so to speak, was her present state of mind.

"It's cold here," she said, as she used to say at the movie house when the air-conditioning had been turned up too high and the film started to lose significant interest because it was only the cold you were thinking about and not the lovers kissing on the screen.

"I wish I had a sweater to give you," I said, knowing it was a foolish idea even as I said it. But one never knows how it is with them or how to treat them, there in their caves of shadows or in the cold mist that embodies them when they come to visit us briefly on earth.

"Don't worry yourself," she said. "I just wanted to say hello, to remind you to cover your uncle's quince trees so that they will not die in the frost."

Sometimes I did forget. I had lost seven of my uncle's trees through my negligence one year, when fall had sprinted to a sudden, unannounced, killing winter.

"That is thoughtful of you, Marie, to be thinking of me and my uncle's quince trees."

"We were friends, weren't we?" she said, her voice trailing off, returning to a faraway place in eternity.

"Friends," I said, rushing to embrace her vanishing mist before it was gone. But it was gone, and without a goodbye.

"Grandma, that was not a good visit," I said. "I'm now worse off than before I came."

She did not hear me, my grandmother, because she was no longer there and neither was I, who was now back on the train weaving its way through Sicily, stopping at every station grand and little, at every village grand and small. The hunter had returned to his seat and the bread eater to his. Each nodded to me, then went about his silent brooding business. The bread eater looked hungrier than ever without his bread, the hunter forlorn without his hares.

"I should have reconciled with your grandmother long ago," my uncle said abruptly, "but then, you know how pride is—harder than granite. And then, when you are ready to make up, it is too late."

Before I could answer, the short Sicilian said, "I should never have stolen that bread. Just for hunger, just for hunger. Now I'm chased all over Sicily because of a few crusts."

Before I could answer either of them, not knowing in fact what to answer them, the compartment door opened with a sly rush. I looked, thinking to see the two policemen reappear; instead the young man with his mandolin entered, flashing us a jackal grin to show us he was friendly.

He began playing a Neapolitan love song much favored at weddings. A tear-jerker it was, sung at the end of the evening, after dinner and dancing and when the wedding guests were in their sentimental cups.

"Across the sea of time I think of you, across the sands of time I think of you, of you, of you, my love," he sang, as the train rattled about from town to town, making no stops.

The longer he sang, the more I began to remember him. Until I finally fixed him as the singer at my own wedding years and years ago. He had not grown older, which was the reason I had not immediately recognized him, because who does not get older with time, with the passing of thousands of weddings and countless other festivities?

If I were ever to get married again, I thought, I would never hire him to sing. Somehow, I blamed him for the souring of my marriage; he had put a bad spell on it from the start. I wondered how many other marriages he had jinxed with the sweetness of his song, with his singing of eternal love that only taunted the gods to do their mischief and shatter all conjugal dreams of joy and permanence.

These were my thoughts as we rode high above the Bronx River, the Botanical Garden in view, burning in the summer heat. My traveling companions did not seem to notice the conflagration, so intent they seemed on their own thoughts and memories. The singer sang away, going from one song to another, indifferent to the fires below and to the heat in the compartment. He had many songs left in his bag, an eternity of them.

I could see now that all the trees were on fire and the river, too, all the flowers in the Botanical Garden and the roses turning into fists of flames, the earthworms and grubs and caterpillars, everything that lived in and above the soil was burning. My grandmother's black dress burst into flames as she was plucking the dandelions from their roots, and the children who were mocking her flared into packages of fire. The Greek temple where my grandmother and I had prayed crumbled under a cascade of smoke and dust, the goddess who had lived there taking flight in some passing clouds. Everything in the Sicily below us was on fire, everything in the Bronx was burning away to ashes, everything but me and their memory.

Self Portrait with Bullfight

For the moment the sky was flat, an uncomplicated gray. Below it, the crowd waved straw hats, the band played, the matadors marched, the bull trotted; she was speaking.

"My love," she said, "this is a honeymoon like no other."

"I'm gratified," I said, "and grateful to your parents for the gift of this trip, the first-class airfare and deluxe hotel included."

"Not to mention the transport to and from the airports— and such incidentals as tips and laundry expenses," she added with the smile of a cash register opening to a large bill.

Cushions and bottles flew over our heads, and loud jeers and other noises of displeasure raged about the stadium and smashed down into the arena and on the actors there, including the baffled bull. In our banter, my bride and I had failed to catch the instant when, in the moment he was about to plunge his sword, the matador had lost his courage and, in a girlishly, son-of-a-diseased-whore sort of way—as the man who had just slipped into the seat beside me described it—fled from the charging bull.

"We're missing a good deal of the action, my dear," I said, to suggest that we might converse after and not during the bull-fight. Talk later, in bed, where kisses sweetly envelope words.

If this marriage was to last, I had advised myself hours before the elephantine wedding a week earlier, forbearance was the key. Passion would come and go, take a cool break and return in hot force, play hide-and-seek, and one day vanish altogether. But with forbearance our life together would troop on bravely and one day perhaps flourish on even more intimate and spiritual terms, ending only when parallel lines shake hands in eternity or with our deaths.

"Would you describe our wedding as elephantine?" she asked, as another matador marched out to finish the job his predecessor had so flagrantly abandoned.

She often read my mind as well as my lips, so it was difficult to conceal from her many of my thoughts, unless I entertained them behind lead walls or from the depths of great oceans or profound cisterns. Or from the commodious, interconnecting caves under sidewalks and streets in the upper Bronx, where my memory was from time to time drifting, even here, now, in Madrid, in the swirl of the *corrida* and the drama of the aborted massacre in the sands below. My mind drifting to those catacombs of Pelham Parkway even when sitting at dinner in the calm, graveled garden of our luxurious hotel—our honeymoon home—in the shadow of the Prado.

"Not at all," I said. "Not a large wedding in the pejorative sense. Large, yes, but in a polished way, like the Taj Mahal or a bowling ball."

"I've come to notice in the past few blissful days that you have slippery propensities," she said, with a face more teeth than smile. "There's something about being in Spain that draws out the unction in you."

"It must be the olives," I said, "and all their oily oil." Indeed, I seemed to be living on olives, plates of them at our hotel, loving especially those olives embedded with almond slivers, an arrangement not found in nature but one creating a new, harmonious structure, at once radical and classical, like the paintings that I loved and wished myself one day to make. Ah! One day, in a world of one days.

"I notice how you relentlessly devour them," she said.

"Well, I wouldn't say relentlessly. Assiduously, perhaps."

"In any case, I sometimes envy the energy and attention you lavish on olives. But mildly so," she added, putting a cushion under her words.

A new bout of catcalls and jeers mounted to the sky and arrowed down to the disturbed arena as another matador fled the scene. My neighbor was distraught again, imploring God to stick the bull up the matador's ass. Then, suddenly, he gave me a hard, punishing look, as if he had suspected me of lifting his wallet or of having committed some low act with his unmarried and only sister. His look would have alarmed me were it not that his left mustache was comically longer than the right and the right was red and the left a searing black.

"Have you ever seen—though I suppose you have seen your share—such shit as this in all your life?" my neighbor barked.

"Never," I said with great authority. Although, in truth, I had never before been to a bullfight or been to Madrid or to the Prado, whose paintings I loved but had seen only in reproduction.

"It's getting chilly," my wife said. "And I can see you are no longer here with me but in some reverie."

"I was dreaming of the joy that is ours."

She offered me her parted lips.

Black clouds stalled above our heads, darkening the arena and threatening to soon make known their views. I was inclining toward her when a giant bag of a cloud sent down a cascade of warm dusty rain.

"Off to the cabs," she said smartly, as my lips were about to plant one on hers.

And soon we were in the street among the other thousands shouting for cabs or rushing about searching for their cars, which were drowning in the black rain. A trolley with snail's horns glided by, stuffed inside and out, but did not make its stop.

"A Sunday born in hell," said my former neighbor in the stands, suddenly materializing beside me. "Have you ever been to hell?" he asked me sweetly.

Before I could answer, my bride said, "We're drowning here."

I offered her my jacket, which had seen the rain of two oceans and several seas, on which I had sailed six in my adventurous and event-filled youth.

"*Muchas gracias*," she said, her generous smile measured to the level of my chivalry.

The crowd was thinning out, disappearing into the city by routes familiar to them and strange to us, leaving us behind in a floating island of three.

"Well," my former neighbor in the stands said, "I can't wait anymore, are you ready for my little ark?"

Ready to go into his car, he meant, what else? His *coche* was close by and he would return us to our hotel or whatever port we wished.

"You look very familiar," I said to his eyes burning in the car mirror.

"I'm a familiar thing," he said. "When you come to know me, I'm even more so, like a wedding cake with nails and ground glass."

Troubling, that image. I tried to mask my apprehension with some pleasantries, offering up the sudden rain and the strangeness of an afternoon in which two matadors had fled before charging bulls. But he was indifferent to the subject of the weather and—considering his outbursts in the stands earlier—dispassionate about the bullfight.

"Life is a dream," he said. "Those matadors were in a dream today that did not include us or the bulls."

"What a wonderful way of thinking about life," I said.

"It's very useful," he said, swerving, just in time, past an open truck heaped with the corpses of dead roses.

He drove in silence and we sat in silence until, without my ever mentioning our destination, he stopped before our hotel.

"Until later," he said, with a grin so wide as to threaten his mustache.

He was affronted when I offered him money and he stayed in a sour cloud of affront even as we said our farewells and thank-yous. But our dark moods were soon dispelled when my wife and I returned happily to our suite facing the great museum.

"Do you know," she said, after we had showered off the rain and dried ourselves with giant white towels, whose cushiony thickness I had never before felt and which I was sure I would never again feel in any world solely mine, "I feel bullish—"

"With your portfolio," I interrupted, "who wouldn't?"

"About our prospects," she continued, disregarding my quip, one informed by many past discussions on financial conditions in the Western world, and especially on her favorite subject, the trickle-down theory of wealth, which proposes that money rains from the lush skies of the rich and filters down to the poor in the desert below, forming an Amazon of bounty to be sailed on by all.

"I think we were fated to see a bullfight where no person or animal was killed, where nothing has died but time. I think we have an omen of our present and future harmony," she said.

"Yes," I said, thinking there is no fate that is not smoothed by the flow of gold, having once known the sweetness that such a flow brings to the everyday table and the nightly bed.

The omens of the saved bulls apart, I found other, mixed signs of our fate waiting for me later at our accustomed table in the garden: an unusually large mound of olives, squirming with hairy worms, on a huge blue plate.

"Ah!" I said, a bit squeamishly. "Here is an ill wind."

"Impossible!" my wife said to our grinning waiter. "It's either the olives or the worms—the combo is out of the question."

"Of course," our waiter said with a deep bow. "I shall remind the chef that we are not in Bulgaria, where these sorts of dishes have their honored place."

"I hope, my dearest husband, that this small debacle has not fouled your present or future mood."

"No, no," I answered cheerily, though the waiter and his sour dish had given me a sense of foreboding. "I'm not disconcerted by this wormy forecast, or any others of its ilk, because long ago, when I was a young man, a woman read my palm and divined my future rosy."

"A woman? A storefront seer, a Gypsy in a wagon?"

"Not exactly," I said, in an uncensored flow of reverie. "Someone dear to me, a mother, a sister—a lover."

What thoughtless, self-destructive mood had possessed me to tell her that, I wondered? And on the third day of our honeymoon? What ill winds would the revelation summon up even on this fair night with a fairer moon?

Indeed, suddenly a great chill swept down from the snow-clad mountains across the street and blew directly over our table and cooled down the garden, inspiring our candles to burn feverishly against the freeze.

"I thought I knew about your loves, and none was a fortune-teller, from what you previously had related."

"Well, my dear," I said, "there are certain things one reserves to tell one's bride after marriage. In any case, I'm not a believer in relating the narrative whole, in one sitting, but in releasing it slowly, advancing and withdrawing, thus not sating my audience in one ecstatic shot."

"You wanted to leave me with some mystery about your person, to keep me enthralled with your impenetrable aura, to savor you slowly over a lifetime, to be the rapt ear to your endless Scheherazade," she said, her voice low.

"Yes, to hold some mystery of myself. To keep you always wanting to know me, for does not familiarity breed contempt—or worse, indifference?"

"Lend me your palm," she said. "I would like to read there a line or two of your life's biography before we repair to bed. I'd like to learn whether I'm even listed in your index."

At that moment, the waiter came with a second plate of olives, more gloriously worm-infested than the first. Worms with childish red lips. I gave him a stern look, disapproving even.

My wife rose to study him. Then, putting on her eye-glasses, which she kept in a silver purse embroidered with natural pearls, and drawing closer to him, she said flatly, "You look most familiar." I seconded her observation.

"We Spaniards all look alike," he said, "especially in cloak-and-dagger darkness, when the flamenco shreds the sanity of night and renders it cuckoo."

"Yes," I said, "perhaps all Spaniards look alike in their brotherhood of despondent capes and sombreros blackened by the night, and with eyes of the same inky shade or related blackish hue, but you look especially familiar."

"I'm familiarity itself," he said, "especially when you know me—then I'm an old ceremonial sword that fits into the sheath of your life, but I'm not a suitable accessory for occasions such as weddings and baptisms. I wear well for funerals, however, especially for those who have died young."

"Oh!" my wife said, warming her hands over the candle flame. "Please do not undervalue yourself, even for rhetorical effect. Life, after all, is a dream, and one may as well dream oneself a prince and not a toad."

"Ah! Yes, I seem to have heard that somewhere before," said the waiter, "an echo from the cave of platitudes." He looked about the garden in search for his words, and with a mean, ironic smile began to utter them: "A sentiment, a sentiment—"

"Beautifully expressed," I interrupted. "And voiced by the kindest of souls."

She smiled at me. The smile of a woman who has at long last found the hero of her dreams. Her happiness, and her happiness with me, drew me into a warm complicity with her: we two, in a garden of surprises and mutual affection. I was, on this frosty night, finding for her a new opening in my heart.

"What a magical night," she exclaimed, "night that stabs the heart with joy!"

"That stabs the heart," the waiter repeated, retreating to the hotel, the tails of his tuxedo jacket trailing wounds in the gravel.

I could see that our waiter had capped the strange events of the day and had put her in a droll mood, one open, I had supposed, to the faraway and the wondrous. I was thus emboldened, perhaps recklessly, to tell her the story of that woman who had read my palm, the story, too, of my former life among the Bronx Gypsies.

"I was a young man," I said, "an orphan—as you know—living in the streets and alleys and doorway pockets."

"How adventurous," she said. "The street, with all its open air, must have made you the great outdoorsman you are—but one with a gusto for a contemplative life, carefree and indifferent to material worries, to matters of daily bread and excellent hotels."

"Yes," I said. "Such a life does build character and stamina for adversity, but it was poor preparation for a life of ease, such as seems to be presently mine."

"So," she said casually, as she snapped a bread stick in half, "this woman, this sister, this skilled lover . . ."

"What is skill in love but the exercise of practiced technique? Passion is another matter," I said, "one requiring a soul."

"So are we talking passion here?" she cried gently, as the mountains sent down yet another blast of ice, frosting our candles altogether. She looked profound in the semidarkness, her blond hair glowing over her eggshell of a face.

"I was talking about the life I once lived long ago, when I was a figment of myself, a fraction of a man, whose dreams had endings but no beginnings and little middle, so that I spent many hours trying to dream their starts, only to arrive at many other new endings. In short, I was at the last stop of a life that had hardly begun. Until, one winter night, when I was deeply asleep, traveling back and forth from one subway terminal to another to keep myself from freezing in the icy city streets, I was awakened by a woman's voice, which I thought belonged to my dream.

"'Wake from this dream,' the voice commanded soothingly, 'and wake into another.'

"And in a flash I was awake and off the train and walking alongside her on an old elevated station whose wooden steps brought us down to a long street of dingy shops and dark restaurants. She took my hand with a grip so gentle that I could feel its hope, and she led me to a shop fronted with barrels of olives and salted sardines, with open sacks of golden grains and powdery condiments, with buckets of flaming red peppers licking the air."

"How bizarre!" my bride exclaimed, like a cat worrying a lace from a fallen shoe.

"Oh! Much smaller, but crammed with bazaar-like items such as hanging golden oil lamps, Persian carpets machine-woven in Taiwan, and patented mousetraps galore."

"Do you think," she said, "that we may order, eat quickly, and vanish into a privacy of two, thus saving the remaining evening for the feast of ourselves, putting aside your tales of wonders for rainy nights and grizzly afternoons—as are sure to come to us in time? My sweet."

"What could make me happier?" I answered, but not so as to seem ironic, as rhetorical questions often do—or when the unconscious is doing its clandestine and dirty work of demolishing the self and its façade of agreeability.

"*Prestoappearo*," I said, making a few complex passes with my hands to indicate that magical words alone were not powerful enough to do the trick of summoning the waiter to our side.

"Did you learn that method of invocation from your days—and nights—with the Gypsy woman?" she asked.

"That and many other secrets," I said, "but I'm bound by powerful oaths not to reveal them."

"How wonderful," she said, "knowing that I have a lifetime to cajole those and other secrets from you. Let me start that prying process tonight, under the cover of soft sheets and softer sighs."

"Yes," I said. "I'm lusting to have my secrets wrested from

me by whatever means you wish, but, as you can see, my occult powers must have waned from disuse, since no application of them has yet produced the waiter."

"You're wrong there, my treasure, because if you turn you may notice his appearance, accompanied by two guests."

"Just a coincidence," I averred, deigning not to seem amazed by two bulls, festooned with garlands of garlic and roses, being ushered to their table.

"It is the custom," our waiter explained, finally returning to us, "to host a banquet for those bulls who survive the day. Of course, they may stay the night, on the house, naturally, and leave when they want and return to their mothers, if they wish."

"What a dream, to return to the warmth of one's mother! Or to her double," I added.

"Oh, dear!" she said. "I see I have failed you, that I have left you feeling adrift in a sea of your own loneliness."

"Not at all," I said, not quite truthfully. "All primordial longings are unresolved infancy, which nothing may resolve so fully as the completion of the interrupted narrative."

"Which completing your story of the Gypsy woman and the history of your youth would satisfy, I suppose."

"More than suppose. It would be the supreme consummation."

"Onward, then," she said with a brave smile, with an affectionate, melancholy salute that one makes to the ship as it sails off, leaving you on the dock.

"To the rear of the shop she ushered me," I said, returning to my story, "and then through a leather curtain and down a gray corridor leading to a gray wall, whose grim stones clearly came from an old demolished prison that had never seen sunlight. There we stood, silently before the cold wall, the world I had left behind already an empty memory, the world ahead nothing but a lifeless stone wall. She moved her hands over the wall, which parted before us, opening to a room bursting with jovial young people boisterously eating at a long wooden table.

"A young man among them called out, '*Hola! Compañero, siéntate, por favor*,' and though until that moment I did not know a word of his language I answered him in perfect Castilian—lisp and all—'*Muchísimas gracias*.' To this day, you may notice, *mi querida*, that my Spanish is flawless, as if I were born to it, which indeed I was, born in the nest of that dining room.

"The young man beckoned me to sit beside him, which I gladly did. Ashillo was his name, he said. 'Ashillo of the moon. For that is how far away my former life is from the one I now live,' he added. He waved his arm over the room: 'How we all live now.'

"He had the haunted, pale face of a man born in a cellar among empty wine bottles, old corks, and piles of coal. He had knives for eyes. We were nineteen, born two days apart, under the same sign of the centaur shooting his arrow to the stars. He was two days the elder but he looked ten years my senior. He understood my surprise when he told me his age.

" 'The prison, the streets, and the prison,' he said with a laugh rinsed through old tears. 'And you?' he asked, spearing a large golden pear with his fork.

" 'The streets, the homes, the streets,' I said.

" 'Now you are home,' he said, in a tone not as welcoming as when he first had greeted me.

"He turned as if to say that the conversation was ended, and left me to myself. I took stock of my surroundings and my companions. More a cave than a room, it was, and lit by golden lanterns strung along braided golden wires and by pearly dots of light embedded in the stone walls. In the flames of candles thick as wrists, our table glowed with golden bowls of waxy green apples born from orchards before the Fall, pomegranates whose ancestors had been plucked by the hands of restless Odysseus and his weary crew, fat dates whose cousins had fed Ali Baba's caravan of forty thieves on desert crossings. Blanched almonds, persimmons, melons, mangoes, pears, and quinces there were, all of no less fabled lineage and provenance. All these stuffs stretched atop a long, dark, ancient wooden table which had borne King Midas's humble plates and bowls before he gilded them with his golden touch.

"Now I could see, too, and for the first time, my benefactress, who had removed her hooded coat, letting fall a sweep of black hair over her rouged white cheeks. She was neither young nor old, neither beautiful nor ugly, but something of a woman who comes into a man's dream when he is drifting on a spar in a shark-driven sea at night, his ship gone down with all hands and heads, his beloved cat drowning, without a cry or a whisker of feline hope, before his eyes."

"I always hoped I was or would become that saving dream," my wife said sotto voce, as if from a well of regret, as if, having landed on the shore of an undiscovered world, she had found a shoe print in the sand.

"That was leagues away in time," I said, "long before my raft drifted into your harbor."

"Your leaky raft," she said, "your raft of discontent, your raft of troubles, your solitary, penniless raft of *Medusa*, if I may say directly and with a tinge of bitterness."

"Raft without sail or rudder," I added, wishing to certify the true nature of my earlier state and to claim my present gratitude for her safe haven. "And knowing that, please understand, then, my happiness when I was welcomed into the Gypsy clan, where there was warmth and sheets and blankets and pillow and a bed, my own, carved at the headboard with mysterious symbols denoting sanctuary from the disquieting world."

"A sanctuary no doubt financed by thieving and tricking, by pilfering and lifting, by con games and gulling, by crystal-ball-gazing and Tarot card readings, by chicken-stealing— all of which I suppose are the Gypsy ways you were taught and blindly followed—blind to the world, as you then were."

"How did we live, you mean?" I thought it best to cast aside her accusations and, lest she imagine my story an invention, a fairy tale without the materiality of cash—the skeleton of all realized dreams—reveal to her the golden underpinnings of our thriving band.

"There was," I explained, "beneath our house and deep beneath the cellar and far into the bedrock, a subtle stream. All the Spanish conquistadores who came to the New World looking for gold had searched for that stream but they had gone in the wrong direction, supposing it was in the lands of the Aztecs and the Incas. But it was not and never was, flowing as it did, slyly, silently underground, a buried stream, an occult tributary of the great Bronx River. A stream flowing with gold flakes, gold dust, and apple-sized nuggets beneath our feet, beneath the floors of the rooms where we ate and slept and dreamed. Gold that we collected in coffee cans and pickle jars, gold that made us rich, but never unpleasantly so. Gold that gave us all good temper and cheer, gold that paved our hearts with the freedom to love.

"I spent my first night alone, in a bliss I never before had known, except for the memory of when my mother suckled me as an infant. But the second night the Gypsy woman woke me with caresses and brought me to her island of a bed, where she fished the loneliness from my heart, adding it to her collection beside that of her lover Ashillo, *compañero* of my first night at the table.

"Of course, I soon adored her, as did Ashillo, who quickly came to hate me for my grotesque manners in bedding his woman without so much as a by-your-leave, hated me for fouling his cushy bed and softer life. I had not deliberately set out to do that to him, I explained. She had chosen me without my knowing it, before I arrived, when I was in a subway car, asleep with my eyes closed dreaming against the world.

"'I welcomed you with good cheer and brotherhood,' he said, 'knowing that she had brought you among us because you were one of us, we who, before her intervention and love, were trash swirling in the gutters.'

"'You are my brother,' I said, reaching for his hand, which he sharply withdrew as if recoiling from a tricky snake. His eyes were blurry with hatred and self-pity.

"'There is no redress for your treachery,' he said, 'unless you leave here and return me my happiness.'

"'Ashillo,' I said, 'let's find a way to resolve this and restore ourselves and our world to harmony.'

"'It is too late for reason and discussion,' he said. I had poisoned his well, he said, I had shit in his orchard, I had murdered his soul.

"We parted, each on his own path of chagrin. But from that day on he devised many ways to make me unhappy, thinking perhaps that I would be goaded into leaving the golden nest and thus return him to his prelapsarian bliss. Once, he shoveled electric eels with fiery eyes and sucking teeth into my bath; once, he ground moldy shoe leather and a powerful emetic into my cereal, leaving me housebound for weeks; once, he planted hallucinogenic drugs under my mattress and called the police, who pocketed them and ordered me to bring them more—as a condition of my freedom. Once, he told my family—as I had now considered the little clan—that I carried several contagious and fatal diseases with fancy Latin names, thus bringing all to shun me like the filthy plague they believed I had become.

"One night, while the others slept, she ushered me and Ashillo into her private library, with walls of books bound in green and red morocco and tooled gold, the carpeted room bathed in the stored light of the full moon, and there she read us several articles of the riot act, which she herself had authored. She had never looked as beautiful as at this moment, with her raven hair sweeping to and fro, at this moment fraught with her injunctions and her fury.

"In sum, she said that there was to be no more rivalry, no more jealousy, no more envy, no more acts of aggression or retaliation or stark revenge by either party. In truth, I had also been guilty of some mischief, such as shredding all five of Ashillo's favorite vintage Hawaiian shirts, featuring guitar-playing frogs riding surfboards in a turbulent tide.

" 'We are not here for squabbles and storms,' she said, 'not here for bickering rivalries and vulgar jealousies, not like those others in the world we want no part of and from whom we have deliberately fled.'

"In short, we were to return to our tranquil, golden days—on pain of expulsion from the family. She had us shake hands like naughty boys, which indeed we were, and make promises of friendship I was sure neither of us intended to keep. So, for a while, we returned to our old routines of love, and the appearance of concord ruled.

"Until one day, that is, when neither Ashillo nor I could bear the truce any longer. I suffered each night I knew she was with him, and he the same when I stayed with her. We were eating our hearts out, what shreds had remained of them. We were each green with black despair, hate seeping through our pores and exploding with each blink of the eye. We suffered, each of us, day by day—and suffered even worse after the fall of light—nightfall, that is, to speak plainly. We sat, among the happy others at the dinner table, like two dogs waiting to be gassed, neither knowing until after the espresso—a bolt of sugar and black lightning—whom she would leave behind for the pound and a lonely death or whom she would choose that night, not knowing our fate until she flashed a smile at one or the other and made a slight nod, as if to say, It's time.

"And then one us of rose and went directly to rosy heaven until morning, when life on earth once again resumed in its ordinary, pleasant, acceptable, agreeably somnambulist way. But I was not happy in my jealousy, however calm the waters had become. That I had been rescued from the grinding subways and the winter ice, from the summer furnace of the open streets, that I had been saved from the sour soup kitchens with their dancing roaches, that I had been spared from the thrift-shop clothes smelling of the recently dead, that my loneliness, like an iron sheet, had been lifted from my heart, now seemed long ago and far away, a story told me in childhood. All my past was forgotten and now I was once again a miserable lad.

"'I'll toss a coin,' Ashillo said one day, the same day and hour when we both had reached the end of our tortured truce. 'Let's finish this once and forever. Whoever loses, leaves,' he said.

"Without a hesitation or reflection, I agreed and let him flip his good-luck charm, an old Iberian doubloon from the time of Calderón and Spain's Golden Age. Up in the air it went, spinning heads tails heads tails tails heads, until it finally landed in his hand, on the wrong side of the world for him.

"'*Usted tiene muy buena suerte*,' he said, with much formality and good grace, I thought; with the murderous dignity of an assassin biding his time, I suspected. But he was a boy of honor and left without a word and disappeared, like a steel blade plunged into the sea.

"My happiness was restored, but within two weeks I missed him and the frisson of our rivalry, which would have been a welcome relief to what now seemed an endless tedium of golden days. He had left without a word of farewell to me or to her, who soon came to me as I was pruning a quince tree in the little orchard behind our house.

"'Have you murdered him?' she asked in a most neutral

way, as if only the information mattered and not the crime that I may have committed.

" 'He is my brother,' I said.

" 'The precedent for fratricide was long ago fixed,' she said, 'so you are hardly unique in its practice.'

" 'Chance took him away,' I said, 'not I.'

"She gave me the look of a distant star, then turned, disappeared into the house, and did not speak or call me to bed that night. But the following day she took me sailing down the East River and far deep into the Narrows, whose vista led to the endless, vacant ocean, where hopes—and for that reason I never look there—vanish at the horizon. She took the wheel while I tended and trimmed the sails, ever puffed with wind, even while the sea all about us lay unrippled, a sheet of becalmed glass. We dropped anchor at noon and lunched on headless sardines, a 1936 Montrachet, and slices of fennel atop blood oranges from Valencia, until, drowsy with repast and sun, we went down to the cabin and, in the tight coffin of the berth, made love silently, in silence."

"Oh!" my wife said, twisting her large napkin. "What a tale. I shall never need or want to hear it or any other ever again, so fabulous is yours, so ripe with rapture and adventure, and for me, so definitive—like a beautiful dream dashed by morning light."

"All that was long ago and far way, an unfulfilled dream of yesterday. But we have before us the open road of the no less enchanting real," I said.

"Filled with potholes and fissures, strewn with broken hearts and old wine bottles of exquisite vintage. I think I'll retire for the night, permanently," she said. "Wake me when the honeymoon is over."

Before I could answer, the waiter, now sporting a dark cloak, appeared with a large bowl of olives, each pierced with a miniature banderilla for a toothpick.

"This should keep you properly engorged," he said most pleasantly. "But careful of the baby *banderillas*, for they are sharpness itself and sometimes silently slide into the stomach, smoothly slicing their way here and there, piercing the peritoneum this way and that, until, before you know it, you are vomiting vast quarts of living blood."

"How kind your caution," I said, as my wife, making a spinnaker of her napkin, rose to sail from the table.

"Leaving before dinner, señora," the waiter asked, "before the main event?"

"I do not much feel like dinner," she answered politely, popping rolls into her napkin.

"Do not leave," I said. "There is more of my story, which, when completed, shall crumble all walls of doubt and restore me to your heart, in whose domain I feel I have been banished and fast disappearing."

She furled her napkin, making a little sling of it, and shot an olive between my eyes.

"This better be a thing of alchemic glory," she said, "a story that can transform antipathy into love." The bulls turned from their dinner, giving me a sympathetic look, as if to say, We who have been reprieved salute you. You who are about to meet the sword.

"We woke," I continued, "from the creamy drowse of love and I thought we would soon make sail and start our return home. But when we were again on deck she said to me, 'Your presence among us will only make me suffer Ashillo's loss all the greater. And I do not live to suffer. I plucked you from your sad dream and now I return you to it. You may come back to us, but only with Ashillo by your side and only when you both agree to abide by our rules of conduct.'

"'Where will I find him?' I asked, with all the alarm of the world in my heart, 'since he has vanished like a sparrow in a fog?'

"'Don't look for a sparrow,' she said, 'look for a hawk.'

"She searched the sky as if looking for a sign of that hawk and then quickly took my hand and read its lines and crevices, its devious roads from birth to death, and declared my future rosy, like dawn before the invention of the steam engine. And with that, she packed me off in a dinghy the size of this table. She herself made her way back up the gray Narrows until she and ship and sail were a raw smudge on the horizon.

"That was the start of my voyages up and down the earth, a vagabond and a searcher, a drifter and a pursuer, an Ishmael and an Ahab, always on the hunt for Ashillo, though taking many off trails and side tracks along the way. Until one day not long ago I came upon you, for whom I have ended all my quests and journeys, for whom I have gladly renounced my dream of returning to those earlier days of bliss."

"Renounce your dream of bliss for a dream of murky commonplace with me, you mean," she said in tones embroidered with lacy frost.

The waiter clicked his fingers, summoning to the table two busboys, whom he ordered to remove all the dishes and silverware and napkins, leaving behind a denuded tablecloth alive with brazen bread crumbs.

"You have enough of dinner," he said, though, in truth, we had not yet finished our meal. "A serenade or two should swell out the rest of your evening and amplify your honeymoonish dreams."

Whereupon he conjured up a guitar and, accompanied by the two busboys for the chorus, began to sing.

"Valencia, in my dreams it always seems I hear you call . . ."

"Please make them stop," she said. "I feel I'm about to feign a headache."

"Oh! Dearest," I exclaimed in a husbandly way, before I passed on her wishes in a voice filled with authority and kindness, filled with good cheer and comradeship for those who work, filled with the slightly imploring whine of the supplicant who knows the odds are against him.

"Valencia . . ." He continued, against my wishes that he cease the strumming and the singing and the obscene grinding that I could see fascinated my bride lewdly but discreetly.

"I think," she said, "our world is coming to an end unless we repair to our rooms—and *muy pronto*."

"Yes! Let's start this night anew, with a fresh slate of our love. But first let me settle my accounts here, the up and down columns our interrupted repast, before I join you in our arbor of joy."

"Oh! Our harbor of joy. Come full sail," she said. "I'll keep the port lights burning. But not forever."

And away she went, in a twitter of stymied romance, her furious stilettos leaving spike holes smoking in their wake.

The singing ceased, the busboys vanished, the bulls—festooned with garlands of spoons and forks—had long disappeared, the night retreated from the tables, leaving only the waiter and myself in a graveled garden lined with folded chairs.

"Well, Ashillo," I said, acknowledging him at last, "you've had a merry time with us in all your protean shapes."

"But you smelled me beneath them all, I'm sure. All disguises are measured by their wish to be penetrated," he said, folding and pocketing his guitar like a deck of cards.

"Well!" I exclaimed, after a considered pause that lasted from the building of the early pyramids to the moment when I set foot in that dinghy years ago and floated out to sea and away from our Gypsy clan and from her. "I have long searched for you, to say that she wanted us back, together or nothing. But as you can see, I'm now installed in another life."

"What other life, amigo—the one you stole from me?"

The stars fell in little crumbles of chalk, stabbing the

screen of the night. I was used to marvels, however, filling my pockets with chalky stars when I was a vagrant youth.

"Don't you find, Ashillo, that all regrets end up in a drawer stacked with calling cards from persons you no longer remember, and thus that it is better to invent new regrets than to refresh the old ones? Why, then, do we not conclude the night with a handshake and a handsome tip for service rendered—the service of your present exit and from our old story of golden days?"

"Or for the life I may save you from?" he asked.

I looked up at my open hotel window as he said that, seeing framed in it my bride in her frilly honeymoon vestments and baked in the fetching glow of dim lights and candles. She was smiling the goofy smile of the bride not sure she had landed her catch—the groom having just walked out for cigarettes, which he never before had smoked. She waved, gold doubloons flowed from her fingertips and scattered at my feet. She was, after all, Midas's daughter, I reflected, but not too deeply, as other matters were pressing.

"Or from the life you have come to take from me?" I inquired, noticing the brace of pistols stuck in his red sash and the dagger between his teeth, not to speak of the notice I took of the little bottle labeled *Poison* rakishly folded like a handkerchief and peering out of his vest pocket.

"Not your life," he said, "but your dreams, which I shall invade day and night, like a rotting red mushroom."

What a prospect, I thought, to have an oozing fungus for

a conjoined brother, one who eats and sleeps with you—and with whomever you are sleeping—until the grave.

"How shall we settle this?" I asked, knowing we would do exactly what we had done in the past, knowing also that all settlements short of death were just reprieves from further and inevitable duels.

"You toss this time," he said, picking up a doubloon from the gravel. "Heads we return to her together; tails, you to your wife and me to my dusty fate."

I looked up again to the window, where my bride was letting fall a coil of braided sheets for me to climb to her. I smiled weakly but with bold intention. She unfurled a sigh, her banner of chagrin.

"I shall toss, Ashillo," I said, a brave guillotine in my voice. "Toss for all it's worth."

I flicked the coin up to the sky—heads tails tails heads, spinning and turning coquettishly, then for a moment hanging like a noose suspended in sluggish time before finally beginning its golden plunge faster and faster back down to the garden of our world.

Self Portrait with Circus

Then I said, "Marie, don't even change. Let's just go and get some dinner over at Romero's."

"What about Eddie?" she said in a voice I didn't appreciate. "Are we just going to leave him here?"

I myself had nothing much against Eddie. Eddie, the bitter midget. He brought along the black clouds wherever he went. Except when he was anywhere near Marie or some other good-looking woman, then the sun came out and he smiled like an infant greedy for his milk.

"Then let's not leave him," I said in the most agreeable way I could muster.

"I can't go like this," she said. "I have to shower and change."

"Sure, if you have to, but I think you look grand the way you are." She was still in her acrobatic tights with a fluffy tutu, pink, like her ballet shoes. She was beautiful and fear-less on the wire, walked it as if in a dream. But that was not why I loved her.

"You're sweet, Louie," she said, "always trying to make me feel good."

"Look, do whatever makes you happy. Shower and change and I'll close down for the night."

"Don't forget to ask Eddie to join us."

"If I run into him," I said.

"Promise?"

"Here's the thing," I said. "If everyone sees us going off with Eddie, they're going to be upset that we didn't ask them. We're going to be stuck with the whole show, even the elephants—you know how jealous they get."

"Those elephants!" She laughed.

The strongman came in the trailer door without knocking.

I had told him a hundred and five times that he had to knock before entering; never mind I was his boss, he did not care what I said or wanted because he was the strongman and they were not easily replaced. Few want to be strongmen in the circus today. They'd rather become wrestlers or bouncers or whatever makes more money and gives more prestige. In my time, being in the circus was a big thing and you ran away from home to be either a sailor or a circus man, not some guy who phonies up a wrestle or stands in front of a club showing off his muscles and thick neck.

"*Hola*, Maria," he said, without looking at me.

"Oh! Hello, Mario," she said with a little stumble in her voice.

He nodded over my way and then followed up with a big fat smile meant for Marie.

"We were just leaving," I said in my most managerial way. He showed me his teeth.

"I made a reservation at Romero's. Just me and you," he said to Marie.

"They don't take reservations," she said.

"They do for me, anytime."

"I hope," I said, "that they will honor a table for one. Or maybe it's not too late for you to invite Marlene."

"She's nice, that Marlene. And she has a big crush on you," Marie added.

He took Marie's hand. "Let's go," he said. "We can work out the particulars later."

"Marie has plans tonight, and they do not include you, Mario."

He turned to me and puffed himself up. "I was talking to a lady," he said. "Are you a lady?" He put his face right close to mine, showing me the black hair in his nostrils.

"Cut it out, boys," Marie said. "And maybe you should get out of my trailer, also."

She had taken off her shoes and hose. Her foot arched high. I had called her feet the pillars of Hercules, so sturdy they were. But with thin aristocratic ankles to match the rest of her high quality. She laughed when I once told her that, but a nice laugh because she was pleased. She once said to me, pointing to the muscles of her arms, "You don't have much here." And then, bringing a finger to her head, "But you got a lot up here."

"In fact," she continued, "now the both of you just leave." She trailed that with, "Please."

"And what'll you do about dinner, Maria, you've got to eat!"

"True," I said, finding a common ground with the muscleman.

"Nothing personal," she said, "but I'll stay in with a can of soup and catch up on my magazines."

She had cozied up her trailer with posters of our tours, so it looked like a comfortable old suitcase from the days when you went across America on trains and took steamers to China. She had built a little kitchen with a hot plate and a fridge that could hold milk for coffee and some kaiser rolls. I could have stayed in that trailer with her all my life.

"That's great," Mario said. "Open a can for me, too. We can relax and I'll read to you. I'm a great reader."

That was enough, I thought. I would have to get him off her, even if I was to take a beating.

"Get out, Mario," I said, "and take your barbells with you. You're fired."

He laughed. "Sure, but first make me leave, four-eyes." He flexed his muscles. Pathetic, I thought. And cheap, too, like his black shoes without laces.

"I'll have security do that," I said, as if not deigning to be sullied by a fistfight.

Marie laughed and he did, too. Then I had to laugh, because Mario was the security when he was not breaking chains across his powerful chest or, to the thrill of the kids, lifting the minivan with the clowns still in it. Our laughing killed the black electricity and left us silent and pouting. Until Marie said:

"Look, you two, give me time to change and we'll all go down to Romero's." And then, as if in afterthought, she tagged that with, "As long as Eddie joins us."

There was a familiar soft swooshing and brushing at the door. I looked out the window and saw there what I had expected, the baby elephant. I went out, but I left the door open so I could keep an eye on Mario while talking with the baby.

He wanted to know if we were going out to dinner. His mother had sent him to ask, he said. How those elephants get wind of things I will never know, but they do. They knew that I loved Marie without my ever saying a word.

"Tell Mother . . ." I said, "tell her that plans are up in the air, that nothing is decided."

"She'll want to know when they are," he said. I could see from the way his ears flapped down that he was embarrassed that he had been sent to run his mother's errands.

"Of course," I said. "Tell your mom and dad that they will be the first to know of any plans." I had meant that because

I admired the elephants and their solid life. Who hasn't ever dreamed being one of them?

I was in trouble now. Because I could not go to dinner without the old couple—they always left the baby behind—and if I invited the elephants to come along, then I would have to ask the lions. That would be bad business: no restaurant welcomed them; even Romero's was touchy about serving them for fear they could not be trusted. Who knows what might get into their lion heads? Just a shrill laugh or the rattle of silver on a plate might set them off to pounce and to devour a diner instead of the steaks before them. Worse, if the lions came, then the dancing snakes had to come or they would go into a coma at performance time. Just lie there in their glass homes pretending to be asleep or sick, lie coiled about each other like a weave of thick rubber hoses. Then they'd go on hunger strike and even if you dumped a host of mice and rats into their glass box they would not stir. People liked the dancing snakes, liked them because they danced. They were a big attraction and I dared not shunt them aside because of a dinner.

I heard a sharp slap and turned. Mario came out of the trailer with a goofy grin. The door slammed behind him.

"Are you happy now?" I asked.

"She touched me—that's more than what you got," he said, stroking his cheek as if to keep the sting of that slap from fading away.

We started walking. They were pulling down the tents and wetting the straw on the ground. The floodlights made the moon pale. The fortune-teller was still at her booth peddling her five-dollar palm readings.

"*Hasta luego*," Mario said. "I'm going back to my trailer."

"I'll walk along with you," I said, thinking he might double back to Marie.

He began to protest. Just then I thought I saw Eddie slip under the fortune-teller's stall and realized that all this talk of going to dinner was nothing without him. So I said, "Fine, but don't let me catch you going back to you know where."

"Boo-hoo," he said, "I'm really afraid!" He still had his hand on his cheek when he turned to leave.

The fortune-teller had on her most enticing Gypsy costume; her blouse was pulled down off the shoulders and her skin was coated with a waxy glow that passed for youth. She did not like me or Marie, so there was no problem of having to invite her to dinner and I did not care at all if she knew about it. I did not like her, either, but she raked in the money and the circus got thirty-five percent from the pile. That paid for a week of the lion's meat with a little change left over.

"A good night?" I asked, wanting to open with something of interest to us both.

"Chicken feed," she said, looking under the counter as she spoke.

I noticed that a giant golden hoop clip-on was missing from

her left ear. She always wore the pair for good luck when she worked.

"Lose something?" I asked.

"Nothing that I can't replace."

"Let's cut to the chase, Marlene," I said. "Didn't I see Eddie slide in here?"

"Did you?" A falsetto voice came from under the counter. The midget crawled out with the earring in his teeth. "Look what I found," he said with a salacious grin. Marlene blushed under her thick rouge.

He was still in his assistant ringmaster's costume, with top hat and white gloves and black whip taller than himself. I had the outfit custom-made for him on a layover in Kansas City, where I had just made him my sidekick in the ring and when he was still full of gratitude.

"We're going to dinner and Marie wants you to come."

"He can't because he's chowing down with me," Marlene said, lifting him to her lap. I thought he might find that humiliating but he gave her a big kiss on the cheek.

"Who else is coming?" he asked.

"The whole crew, the snakes and their minders. Maybe the lions. And Mario, of course."

"Tell Marie I'm busy tonight and anyways she shoulda asked me herself instead of sending you."

"It's just a friendly night," I said. "Everyone's invited, you, too, Marlene."

"Oh! A friendly night." Then, with his teeth slowly pulling

the other ring from the fortune-teller's ear, he added, "Unless she has a better offer, I have another kinda night in mind. Tell her that, why don't you."

"Well, I asked, anyway," I said, feeling a weight off my chest, glad that he would not be anywhere near her. But also worried that without him, Marie would not come to dinner.

I went to the elephant hold and found them milling around, except for Sam, who was sleeping on his feet with one eye open, his trunk drooping with dignity. The baby, his haunches on a bale of hay, yawned and had nothing to say, but his mother came up close to me and in a consoling voice said, "Louie, it's okay whatever happens about dinner. I don't care much for Romero's, anyway."

"We'll find another place the next time we're in town," I said.

"Why don't you bring a sandwich over here, Louie, and we can watch you eat so you won't be alone?"

"Thanks, Mother," I said, and left.

I was on my way to see Marie and tell her that I had looked everywhere but I could not find Eddie. I also wanted to tell her with words what she and the elephants had already known. The moon was black against the floodlights.

Mario's trailer loomed ahead like a loaf of darkness with a little square of light. I went up to the open square very quietly and watched him slick his hair back with an oil whose perfume came through the window like a wind of violets. He combed and recombed and patted down his hair to a shiny wet helmet.

He sang. He was his own guitar. His voice came from a Gypsy cave in Granada, a cave lit by stars and two candles. He sang about love and its miseries and the joy of those miseries. He sang about unrequited love whose remedy was death, but he boasted that his love was even stronger than Death and his steely grip. Then he wrapped a chain tightly about his chest and expanded and expanded himself, his muscles bursting, his face a red furnace, until, at last, the chain snapped, one link following the other.

The Park Near Marienbad

"You say: I never read the newspaper. But I've seen you read the Sunday *Times*. You say: I never go out anymore. But you're out all the time," she said. "You're out with me right now, aren't you?"

"Well?" he said.

"Negative absolutes is what I mean," she said.

"Never is not always negative," he said. "As in, I never not loved you."

He was thin, in a charcoal pin-striped suit too tight for him. Perhaps that was the present style. He had knotted his tie perfectly and tightly in a Windsor—a touch of sartorial rigor to offset the flamboyant effect of the mauve handkerchief draping from his breast pocket. I had seen him in photographs before: the rich Chinese youth of Shanghai in the twenties, with a cigarette poised between the fingers, the eyelids a bit drooping, in the style of the fashionably bored. Or maybe he was more like the gentle young Japanese man whose tender voice dominates the bedroom in *Hiroshima Mon Amour*, one of my favorite of Alain Resnais' films.

She laughed. It was a lovely laugh, full of liking him.

"You do have your ways, from time to time, I must say."

"If you must," he said.

It was an obvious reply, she had set him up so easily. But all in all, I liked their banter. It made me think of a time when lovers were playful, intelligent, before charm took its last waltz with Fred and Ginger, before flirting went pale and faded away. Perhaps I'd misjudged things. Perhaps I was at that stage where life in the past seems more vivid, more beautiful than life in the present.

It was still mild for fall and you could sit comfortably in the hotel's outdoor café, where I sat, close to them, at a small table. They were in their mid-twenties, comfortable—cushioned—in their youth. I gave my coffee a stir from time to time to appear occupied, should they be wondering what I was doing there by myself, alone all that time. My coffee had long grown cold. I never could understand the expression—shouldn't one say devolved or declined, descended or degenerated into coldness?

I tried very hard never to look at her directly. I wanted to very much. Wanted to be invisible and regard her forever—for at least three hours, while she read a book on a stone bench

in a mazed garden with hedges climbing to the moon. Sometimes she would gently raise her left shoulder to emphasize a
point, or to accentuate weariness or annoyance—as if to say,
Yes, yes, whatever you say, but now, please, leave me alone—a
gesture Delphine Seyrig made famous four decades or so ago
in Resnais's *Last Year at Marienbad*.

When the film first screened in America, when I was still
such a young man, I told my friends I would fall in love with
the first woman I saw make that gesture in real life. But then,
one day, not long after, I did fall in love, but with a woman
who never raised her shoulder, never tilted her head when she
laughed or even seemed to move her lips when she spoke.

She ordered her third caffè macchiato—"Just the thinnest
streak of coffee, please." She smiled at the waiter, giving him
her upturned, full face, and smiled again as if to say, Trouble
yourself on my account, only if you feel disposed to.

"I've never seen you drink so much coffee," he said.

"I always drink so much," she said. "Where have you been
the last three years, Charles?"

"Never without you," he said, "even when I'm not with you."

"And always faithful, of course?"

"Never not," he said.

They glanced my way once or twice, and later, on the third
look, they turned to meet each other's eyes, as if to ask, Who
is this man and why is he eavesdropping? I may have imagined it, feeling a bit embarrassed at being thought a busybody
and maybe worse. I paid the check. I never wanted to leave the

table while they were still there, but how much longer could I stay without seeming an open coffin in the living room? I rose to leave. The man she called Charles smiled at me, I thought, and she gave me a friendly nod, I thought. Maybe I just wanted to imagine their being friendly to feel better about my sitting there like the besotted old fool in Visconti's *Death in Venice*.

Another Sunday. Less exciting for me than Saturday for touring galleries and museums, when I always feel the thrill of squandering the day on art. But Sunday, when the weekend is reaching its terminal border, I didn't care how it burned down, as long as it burned quickly and the day soon vanished behind a Monday, the start of the consequential world.

The trees were still green and further shaded Central Park in its stretch of afternoon light. Poussin would have known how to render the blackish branches and the pockets of shadow among the leaves and the caves of dusk leading far into the park. A few young painters today might do the same, if they dared to be thought quaint. A lively traffic of people were climbing and descending, winding through the clusters of sun worshippers sprawled on the steps of the Metropolitan. In all my years of my climbing and descending those steps I never had the same count going up as I did down. I explain that as yet another mystery of life.

Mysteries of all sizes abound, of course. Sometimes, for instance, I wonder if my wife and I had loved paintings less would we have had more friends or perhaps even had children—

or both. Though I've noticed that having even a few of the latter means having fewer of the former. Maybe that was just true for our circle, people who gave their lives to raising children and working hard to pave their way—the children's, I mean. Would they have children, those two? I'm sure they had friends, beautiful like them, young like them—immortal.

There were paintings across the street and up those trafficked steps I had earlier thought to visit before the day's end, but I decided to stroll through the park for a while for a taste of nature and maybe a peek into the zoo and—should they still have them—its elephants and their broad, leafy ears. What would life be without ever seeing them again? Never to see the elephants again. Never to smell their dusty gray hides as they brushed against the bars of their prison, never to smell their rich manure, spread like milky brown cakes along the cage floor. I would miss the trees in the park, too, and the various lights of day and lights of seasons and the various weathers wending through them. So much to miss.

How long a list would it be, my list of missing?

Then on second thought, I decided to visit the paintings before doing anything else. I would miss them more than the trees and the elephants; it would be better to see them first should anything unexpected happen to me in the next hour or so while walking through the park. Should an old Mosler safe fall from a tree, say, and land on my head before I had made my way back to the museum to visit the paintings I loved—my reliable old friends on the walls. I was accustomed and sometimes maybe even a bit bored with those friends but they would not suddenly become banal or aggressive, or turn chilly when you went, full of warmth, to pay them a visit. They would one day die, molder and disintegrate like all things made of cloth and paint, but then so would I. But, reassuringly for me, well before them.

The Poussins were not the best. The Met didn't have the best, in any case. So why make a point of it? Unless it is to say that I wished to be seeing again the paintings of his I love at the Prado or the Louvre and to be there with her again, where we had spent a life of Sundays—especially in the fall—in a life of years together.

The statues of the archaic couple in the garden at the Marienbad spa, where the attempted seduction takes place, were, I'm told, adapted from figures in Poussin's paintings. The beautiful Delphine Seyrig is standing beside those statues when she turns to her seducer, placing her hand on her raised shoulder, and says, "No, we did not meet there, not here at Marienbad—not anywhere." Along with the elephants and the trees and the paintings, I would never see that film—or any other—again.

Perhaps that young woman would walk in the gallery without her lover and smile at me as she had at the café, and if she had—would I go to her and ask, Do you remember our meeting here last year? Here, by the Poussins, in this very room? Of course, I never would speak to her, knowing we had never met. Knowing, too, that as I grow older I have become increasingly shy to approach women, to talk to them, even after we have been introduced—properly introduced, as we once would have said. I never would speak to her but would leave her to enjoy the paintings alone, even though she had smiled at me.

Not the best Poussins in the world, as I have said, but they would do for a lingering glance or two—a glance of three. A glance of three is just my steal. In one of his films, Groucho says, "I'll tell him a thing or two—a thing a three."

My wife often said, "Do you have to footnote everything you steal?"

"I'd rather be thought unoriginal," I'd answer, "than be thought a plagiarist."

"How very noble of you," she'd say.

She had been a trial lawyer and a bit on the hard side when it came to softening the language. She thought mine needed toughing up, a little more steel and less equivocation. "Less trying to be fair," she'd say. "It's boring to be fair all the time."

Poussin was a fair man. Temperate, which is a way of being fair. Excess in art is intemperate, a form of special pleading, like that of a trial lawyer's single-minded and driven insistence in nailing down a point, whatever the point.

He married the seventeen-year-old daughter of a couple who had nursed him to health, when he was very ill—the French disease. He was faithful to his wife for the thirty-four years of their marriage, Poussin was; meaning that he was fair to her until she died. Maybe he did not love her excessively and that made it easy—or easier—to be fair. Or maybe he found in his reading of Montaigne's essay *"Sur des vers de Virgile"* confirmation of his own fidelity to his wife, to his painting, to a life of fairness. A life of companionate ease that had begun in friendship and ended in love. A marriage that begins in erotic attraction does not last long, Montaigne thought. Poussin must have locked Eros in his studio before he went home each day to his wife. But in the end, what does it matter whom one has loved or how; there is no nostalgia in the grave, I would say, but for its obviousness.

Temperate and balanced Poussin was, especially in his art, where he worked to make everything fit aesthetically and emotionally, to be sure that nothing in the painting cried out too loudly, some raging color, say, or a discordant shape that threw the painting off-kilter and, like an anvil, weighed down the canvas. He had spent his life arriving at that balance.

But what was the balance worth, then, when one day, in Rome, after a long and bountiful life of work and a year after his wife had died, he got sick again and this time there was no one to heal him? When Death came, I wonder how fair Poussin felt was his visit. Did he try to explain that it was not fair, his dying, because he had led a temperate life and had been a faithful husband, that he had injured no one, especially in his art? Did he explain all that? Did he argue for more time in which to make more beautiful paintings, reconciling all disharmonies, thus bringing even annoying Death into the circle of life's sweet dance? Did he think he would be granted a reprieve?

All these thoughts came and went until I finally decided not to climb those steps and not to visit again those paintings, which I have seen so many times. The young woman would not be in the museum, in any case, and if she had come, she would not have come alone—and, of course, I would not approach her, however much I wanted to, and I never would have said: Haven't I seen you someplace before, at the Prado or the Louvre or at Marienbad?

Or have said: I know you were studying me at the café and I understood that you were fascinated by what you recognized. I realized when you walked in here that you had, under some pretext, left your lover and followed me here, hoping that I would say to you exactly what I am now saying, which is: I loved you before you were born, have waited for you to be born, went to that café today waiting for you to sit there and order three caffè macchiatos—with just the thinnest streak of coffee— and to see me and to recognize in me, beyond the mask of my years, the man you have been expecting even before you came into this world. And what if she had said: Yes, exactly. That is why I'm here. And what if she had raised her shoulder and added: Must I explain further? How would I have answered? I took to the park with a good laugh at myself. Before I became an old fool, I was, I suppose, just a fool.

Sometimes, I thought, had I liked paintings less my wife might not have died. A kind of literary punishment on me.

"Sometimes I think that you can't experience anything unless it's mediated by art," she said once, after we had finished a dinner she had cooked.

"Well, what is a life unmediated by art?" I asked. "All civilized life is mediated by art," I threw in for good measure.

"Was this a civilized dinner?" she asked, a bit tartly, I thought. "Or was it an uncivilized dinner unmediated by art?"

I could hear her legal mind getting ready to trap me in a line of interrogation, and I was trappable, as my experience with her had proved time and again.

Not that I loved her less than art, but that in my eyes she—like the dinner—was mediated by art, was what she meant—and would soon get me to confess. The roast and the al dente greens and the wine would all lead me there, if we delved into the topic long enough.

I made the case that the cultivation of the grape is historically linked to the origins of civilization and hence to art—like wine, another nonutilitarian by-product of culture—thus inadvertently proving her point about me. I confessed. I feigned repentance, made promises to change. I would try to see the food on the plate as food and not an arrangement of this color and that form, and to see her nakedly, without the screen of culture—clothing especially—between us. I liked the way she did combat with ideas and how I would always be brought to lose my case. I liked that at the end of our fruitless debates we would make love, as if that had been the goal of our debate all along, lovemaking, unmediated by art.

Never to lift her thigh, to part the lips, to see her smile and feel her arm about my neck. Never to see a curious cloud drift by the window as I raised my head from her at the mad moment of coming. Never to make love again. Always to be dead. Of course, you won't know what you are missing because you'll be dead, I'm told. Of course, that may be true, but I'm missing now what I shall miss then; I'm missing, you might say, prospectively. If we were to argue again in a museum or in a café or again walk toward the unmediated bed, I would now tell her that art is an inventory of missing.

Families were leaving the park, going home. Couples, too. To a movie, maybe, or to catch something on TV. Or maybe to dinner and then to bed. The pigeons, naturally, would stay behind. I had been daydreaming so long that it was too late to change my mind again and visit my old friends fixed on the walls. Still, I was happy on the bench, in the fading light of a day I would one day miss.

Someone was standing over me, speaking to me. He had seen me at the café earlier and was too timid to ask whether I was so-and-so the art critic. I was he—all day, I quipped. I had reviewed his last show, he said, introducing himself, his tie still tightly knotted.

"Favorably, I hope?"

"You were filled with admiration," she said. "'He does not torture the paint,' you said." She placed her hand on her boyfriend's shoulder and smiled.

I had liked the phrase and had waited for the occasion to

work it into a review. I was glad I had written a laudatory review, though I had liked the work less than what I had written. With young artists, it is better to give them some slack and a little hope. There would be plenty of knives to come later; if they kept on working, that is.

I still could not look at her directly. Though when I did, I felt as if I had walked through a narrow dark path bordered by gloomy tall hedges, the lights of a chateau behind me, and I suddenly emerged in a wide sunny field running down to the bluest Mediterranean. Puvis de Chavannes and Cézanne had named that sea a watery Eden and Godard had made it a sea of jealousy in *Contempt*. And now I was a voyeur in those seas.

She was a painter, too, he said. I was glad that he had spoken up for her; it made me like him better, though I would have been happiest if he had vanished or had never appeared. Or better, had never been born.

"I'd love you to see my work," she said. I was waiting for her to raise her shoulder, but she did not. Perhaps she did that only for him.

Perhaps, as she was not currently showing, I would one day visit her studio, she added. Her directness had a kind of shy bravery to it.

"Of course," I said, giving her my office number. I had done the same hundreds of times before. I had never returned the calls hundreds of times before. We shook hands; he made a slight, elegant bow, wholly out of time, and so lovely. I could never pursue her guiltlessly in this or any other garden after his show of elegance, though I could, in the future, conjure up her face and her captivating gesture. I could wait for her call and never return it, and imagine her among the inventory of items that I would miss.

I gave them time to leave and then started home in no hurry. I had some wonderful books waiting for me by my bed, books I had pretended to have read but for years always kept postponing. Spenser's *The Faerie Queene*, for instance, and Milton's *Paradise Regained*, for another. Even if I read them, there would be others I would never have time to read, leaving me with that regretful sense of never having lived.

She loved books, too, my wife, but she always said she would take a movie or a cigarette over a book, if those were her only choices. She smoked a lot. Paintings were a different matter. She would travel with me anywhere to see a painting or a mural. The original entranceway to the Boston Public Library, for example, where we went one weekend to see, mounting the stairway, Puvis de Chavannes' frescoes: stocky olive trees dotting a Picardy forest, in an age of iron axes.

I commissioned her portrait for our twenty-fifth anniversary. It is still in her room with all her other things—her clothes, and her telephone, too, which I could never bear to disconnect. Sometimes her phone rings late at night, a client on the other end who had not ever gotten the news. She would take calls at any hour. I could hear her across the hall chattering away about some case and would wonder why she was not chattering with me, her lips hardly moving. Then the conversation would end and she'd come into my bed and say, "Is there any room for me?"

"Never," I'd always say.

She was in a tailored wool jacket, arm resting on a book whose title showed distinctly: Racine's *Oeuvres complètes*, a book I had given her and which she always had intended to read, in French, intending, also, one day to learn that language. It was a banal portrait, without the fervor of its subject. But I liked the way the artist had caught, through a few daubs, the nap of her sleeve. He had a talent for detail and none for the whole. Though in one detail, her smile, he captured her fully. A pleased smile, as if to say, at the end of her summation, I rest my case.

At the end, I would like to say those same words for the summation of my inventory of everything I shall miss when dead. Sometimes I imagine a judge enjoining me to limit my list to just ten. The ocean at dawn, I might start with. Hearing my wife say, "Don't turn off the light, just yet," is another. To feel the snow wet my face as I look up to see a changing stoplight. I'd be beyond my ten in no time.

I have no ready order of priority. But I would soon set about to list every particle in the universe: every quark, neutrino, and atom, naming each one as they bounce and shoot through the world. The stars and the galaxies, too, and the gases they bake in. I would list not only every tree throughout the globe, giving a name to each, but also give a name to every plant and leaf and stem, to every raindrop, cloud, fog, mist, dew, and to every mineral, crystal, stone, grain of sand, to every amoeba, whole and dividing, spirogyra and paramecium, as well. And sounds: whispers, squeaks, cries, groans, roars, hisses, barks, clinking, the fall of shoes, symphonies, string quartets, quintets, trios, and solos. Have I mentioned the stars and galaxies? Them, too.

I would list every painting in every museum and gallery. Paintings still wet in studios and paintings hibernating in attics. Have I included all the marks, scratches, and drawings humans have made on walls of caves and prisons? I would not forget the frescoes in Italian restaurants and pizza parlors—gondolas in a Venetian canal, Vesuvius in flagrant eruption, moonlight on the Bay of Sorrento.

I would always remember the movies. All of them—the silent ones and those voiced in every language. From the first mute screen kiss to the thundering stampedes of 3-D cattle on western plains. I would miss them all, but especially the film in which the mysterious woman the narrator pursues is bound to him by an immortal loop of repetitions and in which he is linked eternally to her by hopes endlessly unfulfilled and endlessly renewed.

Self Portrait with Cheese

The sardines were not forthcoming, not to be brought forth, the waiter announced. Plenty and various breeds of cheeses to be had; olives as well, hard ones, with little pimento eyes. Martinis, for sure. Young ones, smoking with cold. But the sardines were to remain on their shelf, entombed in their oily tins, not to see the light of day. Or any light, whatsoever.

"And the salmon? Are they running free now?" I asked cautiously. Best to be cautious about the salmon, they are so sensitive to inquiry. Especially from bears and men with magic wands wading in cold streams, but there was no need for them to fear us, as we were far away, across from a museum, in a hotel garden, under a red umbrella, beneath a toothless sky.

The waiter was indifferent to the salmon, had no thoughts

about them, he said, as they did not swim in the current menu. He was a fancy-talking waiter, who nursed us after we devoured the day devouring paintings. It was a strenuous life, if you were not built for it.

"I guess I'm not beautiful at all," she said. "But then again, who knows what that means these days? Do you?"

We had been talking, before the waiter arrived, about beauty, its properties, its various manifestations in art. Before I could answer, she asked, "Is a slice of cheese beautiful, a work of art?"

"It depends," I said, rather hastily, "on the color and texture and size, whether or not the surface is interrupted with perforations, and, of course, there's the factor of 'whatnot.'"

"The 'whatnot' is crucial, of course," she said. "But what I mean is can a slice of cheese with all its 'whatnot' be considered a work of art, a slice of cheese deliberately sliced in a slicer or carved with a knife—not just some accidental hunk broken off a wheel, if you get my obvious point?"

"Well, if the cheese evokes your appetite, that would immediately exclude it from the category of pure art," I said, repeating some long-forgotten formula. But I was soon filled with regret because I knew in my heart that art could evoke a desire for love, for life, for food, for death—for all that, all at once.

"I was once beautiful," she said. "I was the cheese and you my plate, and individually and together we were beautiful. But I'm not beautiful now, alone or *ensemble*, right?"

"No, not beautiful," I said. "But still beautiful, in a desirable sort of way, if you know what I mean."

"So something that was beautiful in one way can become beautiful in another way?"

"Perhaps, in your case," I said, "but maybe not in any other. You may be the one exceptional and immutable and unique instance," I averred, not too pontifically, not too diffidently, either, but with friendly authority.

"Well, you slipped out of that one," she said. "But you can't say that I'm especially clever or bright or talented at anything—or even with a body that makes men dream searing erotic dreams, a body that shatters memory and convulses reason."

"That's true," I said, with great purity, with great grace, a gliding salmon in a pristine river high in untracked mountains, in America, in 1850, when the New World was still new, in Albert Bierstadt's imagined golden West, a river falling into some giant frothing cascade arched by redwoods taller than cathedrals, higher than belief.

She thought for a while, or seemed to be thinking. Then she said, as if having made a discovery, "And with no compensating charm to compensate."

"None very much," I said.

"What about money? Do I have money?" she asked her martini with its drowned olive.

I waited, discreetly, for her to address the question to me before answering.

"Well," she said, finally looking my way, "do I?"

"Some, but not enough to attract vivid interest."

"There you are!" she said. "I have nothing to recommend me. Not even in your eyes. And you say you love me?"

"I do."

"You say you do, but do you?"

"More than ever, more than never, more than mirrors, if you get my meaning."

"Wait! I'm not even any longer young."

"Of course not. Youth left you years ago. Fled you, I should say."

"So, you are leaving me, too, then?"

"Unlikely."

"Don't you have any principles? Any aesthetic? Any point of view, any taste, so to speak?"

"Let's change the subject," I hinted suavely. "Let's go for a walk. Let's go for a swim in some lake or river or creek. Someplace untracked and undiscovered, someplace where bears have never slept in winter, someplace mirror-smooth and unscratched, like a tabula rasa of the heart."

"What if I grow a beard?" she asked. "Would you still love me then, with a great black beard hanging down my chin?"

"Have I ever denounced your little mustache?" I asked, as if taking offense.

"Not to my face," she said. "Speaking of that, have you seen yours lately?"

"I can't find a mirror to reflect it," I said. "I look in a mirror and see a mirror."

She took me in very carefully, scientifically, so to speak, this way and that. Then, adjusting her eyeglasses on her bumpy nose, she said, "I look at you and do see a mirror, but not my reflection. What kind of mirror is that?"

"A paradoxical one," I said.

"What is the world coming to?" she said, in a dreamy, melancholic, and finally judgmental kind of way that implies that the world is coming to no good and will arrive there soon. To come to no good, meaning what? I wondered. To come to no conclusion I would wish for, I answered myself.

"Wait!" she said. "Does that mean you can't find a mirror to reflect your face or that no mirror reflects your face?"

"It means both," I said. "*Toot la der.*"

"I love when you speak French," she said. "It makes me . . . it makes me . . . it makes me think."

"Makes you reflect, so to speak, in the Old World Cartesian way that bores me to death and makes dreamers yawn even in their deepest reverie?"

"In the Old World way," she said, paraphrasing me, "where mirrors, pools, and all reflecting surfaces have their mystery, which I wish I had more of, at least for myself, personally."

"Lots of reflecting surfaces in Cocteau's films," I noted, didactically, but cautiously so. "Though the films seem a bit stale now, as no one finds walking through smoky mirrors so mysterious or miraculous any longer. That's what the world is coming to, I suppose."

"I like best his film where the Beast is in love with the Beauty. Somewhat like our own story in reverse, *nest pa*?" she added with a cheery sadness.

"*Say vray*," I said.

"I'm very fond of you anyway," she said. "Love you, even. Like a broken-winged seagull still longing to fly, still yearning to skim the waves and climb high above the spume."

"And into a wall," I said.

"I'm fond of your juxtapositions, cruel as they are," she said, "because I'm also fond of their true sources in such artists like Max Earnest and Salvador Dolly, in addition to artists I'm sure you've never dreamed of, dwelling as you do in the atmosphere of received and not too complex ideas."

"How insightful," I said, not too critically or too haughtily or too arrogantly or too snobbishly or too sarcastically or ironically, even. But with the dignity of a retired eagle on vacation, gliding above great smoggy, snowcapped cities.

"Wait! See! I'm not even especially insightful."

"Very perceptive," I noted compassionately, like the Buddha regarding the great snake finally swallowing the world.

"But you still love me?"

"*Sand sess.*"

"When you speak French," she said, "I think: Surrealism. Think of the irrational, the unconscious, the world of dreams, of André Breton's 1924 *Manifesto*, of the deliberate flight from reason and logic, of the abrogation of gravity, of all syntax, visual and linguistic, of Newtonian physics, of love on horizontal planes, of everything that makes the world the wonderful goofy place it is."

The waiter brought over a platter of sliced eyeballs, a gift of the house, in lieu of the sardines, he said, and then he said again. We were not sure whether to salt or pepper them or salt and pepper them or to add a drop of lemon, but then, the world was wide with implications and the evening still filled with vacant empty hours ahead.

"You neither salt nor pepper them," he said, as if reading our minds. Indeed, he had read our minds, being the perfect waiter, the waiter of one's dreams.

"They go well with fresh tears, not too many, however, and tears not born from sadness or welled up from existential chagrin or worldly disappointments," he advised.

"There is something rare about these eyes," she asserted timidly, poking at the heap with her fork, the salad one, shaped like Neptune's trident.

I agreed, these were delicate, translucent, not like the thick sheep's eyes I once ate in the Atlas Mountains, where they were served to me as a delicacy greater than salt gleaned from the mist of dreams.

"Of course," the waiter said. "I was sure you would notice their rarity, each eye plucked from the forehead of a baby Cyclops, so hard to find these days of Homeric disenchantment. I suspected from the first moment that you both had qualities of discernment," the waiter said. "Exceptional," he continued, "in the perception department—abstract yet rooted in things or thingness."

"Quiddity," she said, the more precise word. "Indicating the essential nature of things in existence."

"There are no essential natures, as all is mutable and transformative, except God," he said, giving to an ant wandering from its red troop a warning flick of his belt.

This is a fine and novelistic close of the day, I thought, the evening blending the gastronomic and the philosophical. Soon, memories real and imagined, adventures and journeys in the same vein were sure to follow.

"Let's leave," I commanded suggestively. "There is too much active activity here, too much discourse, one wayward ant too many."

It wasn't the ant, actually, but the telescope he was carrying on his shoulders that had disconcerted me. A tiny telescope, of course, midget-sized, to suit an ant's ambition, one broader than mine, I was sure, because mine had winnowed down to sitting in a garden by a vast museum, while the ant's scope was vagabond and, considering the heavy instrument he suffered himself to carry, filled with celestial curiosity. For some while now, I noticed, I was going flat, like a white silhouette one slips under the door or between the pages of a book.

The waiter presented our chit, which I signed with a toothpick prick of blood, as evidence of the gratitude for the exquisite service, for the gift of the eyeballs, which were already melting into a gelatinous little mountain on the plate. Like the mountain where once I lived in a cave, the home of a family of black bears escaped from a circus.

"Have I ever told you about my time in a bear cave?" I asked her absentmindedly, my mind being absent from the concern of whether or not she had ever heard me tell my story, so concerned was I, at the moment, with what finally had ever become of those bears, who had smelled so richly of dark Belgium chocolate.

" 'Art must be convulsive or nothing at all,' " she said. "Is your story convulsive?"

"I'm not sure," I said obliquely, "but I know it bears telling. Or more truthfully, I can't bear not to tell it."

"Ha! Ha!" she whispered, like a mouse at vespers. "Well, then, I won't bait you any longer: begin," she said expressively but without much feeling. And so I began from the beginning.

"They had deserted the circus, these bears, though since they had not voluntarily joined I can hardly say they had deserted it; had fled from it, I should say."

"Wait! Is this just another mama, papa, and baby bear story, with bowls of steaming porridge?" she asked, interruptedly, inopportunely, impolitely, along with several other words beginning with *i*, I thought.

Ignoring the intrusion, I recommenced: "They had been leading a happy beach life, so to speak, deck chairs, large umbrellas, icy waters in rapid rivers falling from mountains, where they lived in bucolic, familial isolation, in a commodious cave, carpeted with pine boughs and delicious downy bark, when they were plucked from their steady bliss by a band of circus slavers, who trucked them to a small city on the western coast. Where they were trained—under methods that included electric shocks and beatings with a hickory stick—to ride tricycles, and to walk, upright and daintily, holding children's parasols aloft; to walk to and fro on tight wires high above flaming walls of fire.

"For some years, they endured all, restraints, beatings, hunger for their customary springtime salmon freshly pawed from the stream, endured the stink of stale hay and piss-soaked sawdust, suffered tight cages and tighter costumes, designed to make them resemble a family of humans, with pants and dresses and porkpie hats and suburban manners.

"But nothing, not the dull, mealy meals, not the punishments for disciplinary infractions, not the stupid clothes, the crushing cages, nothing merited their displeasure as did the routine of their acts. Boredom grand, soporific, and dull: the tricycle ride, round and round; the tight-wire walk, back and forth and forth and back; the bear family at high tea with an uninspired midget lady dressed as Goldilocks, blond mop of a wig trailing over her face. 'Help us!' they cried. But there was no one to help them: the lions, elephants, the seals, the chimps, each had his and her own universe of problems, performancewise, and otherwise."

"Oh!" she said, in a tone expressing sadness. Then, brushing a pear-sized tear from her cheek, she added, "What a trite story."

"There is no pleasing you," I said. "Nothing in fact or fiction will do, I suppose."

"Your head pleases me, or the mirror it has become," she said, "it pleases my eyes, because, happily, as you were telling your story, the mirror has come to include me, while leaving out the rest of the world."

"Did you notice that?" I said, suddenly moved to the legendary border of desire.

"Did you think I would be so obtuse, so blind? Though I must admit my eyes no longer have that brilliant sparkle and diamond gleam of yore?"

"Does this mean I may continue my story?" I asked, eagerly waiting for her answer, but knowing beforehand her reply. But before she could answer, I pointed to the sky, indicating the sudden appearance of herring clouds. Swimming, they were, in graceful little schools, unlike the cumulus clouds, which just drift along like stupid, puffy blimps, relying on their mass, as did the biographer of skies, Tiepolo, for dramatic effect.

"Related to the sardines," I instructed, having them on my mind after seeing, that day, *Burial of the Sardine*, Goya's painting of ecstatic revelers at their festival celebrating the interment of that little fish, making me want to see some, sleeping in rows in their oily tin coffin. Thinking, also, that I would bury a tin or two and resurrect them as little oily paintings.

"Being in the same fishy family herrings are," I continued. Of course, all the meteorological info was a rhetorical trick of suspense, to keep her hungry for the continuation of my story. I had many such tricks up my sleeve and in several locations elsewhere, to keep her on the edge, so to speak and so to speak.

"Darling," she said, "I think I've heard enough of this wonderful tale for the day—and the evening, too. If you don't mind."

Sometimes, I have noticed, a person has to be in the mood to be tricked. Or needs a heavier grade of oil. So I tried again.

"Actually, it would hurt my feelings not to continue," I said, pointing this time not to the sky but to my heart, or rather to the general area under which it was invisibly doing its work.

She leaned back in her chair, a hank of blond hair falling over her face like a golden tail over a dry bone. A dry white bone with one eye that saw through mirrors and intentions. Leaned back, as if to say, Continue if you must, but don't mind if every so often I gaze up at the sky to marvel at the herrings in their thin sea. I took the hint gracefully—manfully, I suspect they would have said in olden times—and I braved my way ahead.

"They were very unhappily bored, those bears, and, to make the story short, one night they escaped the cages and the circus itself." The details of their escapade I held back for another time, another garden, another city—perhaps for another woman, one more easily aroused by tales of devil-dare and derring-do.

"Fled the towns and villages and the sandy coast and straight up into the mountains, where they soon found a new cave for their home, one as deep and cozy as their last and in even a more remote, desperate region, shunned by campers and other thrill seekers. There they settled down and began their new, free life. Just the three, except for me, who, lost in the mountains and starving and desolate, was amazed, when, just as I was ready to give up the flesh and let my soul decide its own way, I stumbled upon the family of bears drunk on berries and honey.

"In a little clearing by a rapid stream they were, half awake and half in the lazy drowse of their inebriation, and belly-up in the sun filtering gently through the pine branches. They quickly discerned that I was not a hunter or bear-catcher, that I was a solitary, lost being, myself wary of my own kind— humans, that is—and happy to have run into them and not a tribe of dancing, mouth-frothing green snakes, so abundant in those wild regions.

"They took me in, literally. Gave me a corner of their cave and a bed of pine needles, and they let me share their food—the water I drew myself from the cold, so cold, and so clear stream. They smelled of chocolate, as I remarked earlier, smelled like giant chocolate bears you would wish to take a bite of. So comforting their aroma, at night, when we all went to sleep, when I wanted something familiar of home to reassure me that I myself had not become a bear, a wild animal who had once been trained to perform stunts, to entertain.

"Slowly, I learned that they could speak. Not loquaciously, not fluently, not with a broad vocabulary, not with nuance, but well enough to say what they wanted to say and to send their thoughts to me across the dark cave. Ursula Minor, as I called the baby bear, was the least articulate and perhaps the most mature in thought. Ursula Major, the papa, spoke most directly, but without subtlety. Ursula Mater was the most rounded in speech and mind, and the most attractive of the three, with a silver streak running down her furry cheek.

"Theirs was a happy home. The salmon ran like water. Berries dropped into their mouths, the honey was inexhaustible and the bees careless. They liked each other, admired each other's integrity, were glad to be a family. But they were growing bored, growing despondent, sometimes even glum. My unexpected appearance gave the lift that novelty gives, but after a month of me the novelty wore thin, like a holiday alone in bed.

" 'Bored,' Ursula Mater said, because in some sense they were no longer the same bears as before they joined the circus.

" 'Joined?' I asked.

"Of course, they had been abducted, kidnapped, hauled off. But they had picked up the expression 'joined the circus,' meaning to trade a staid world for an exciting one, and the term seemed to befit the mood they currently were in.

" 'How much salmon can we eat until we are gorged and sick of salmon?' Ursula Mater asked. 'We hardly have to dip our paws in the stream and there they are, thick, fresh, juicy, ready to slide into the mouth. Ditto with the berries and the honey.'

" 'And then, what?' Ursula Major added. 'We lay about, roll about, lounge about all day, then take a dip in the hottest part of the afternoon, and then laze about again in the shade.'

" 'That's a bear's life, Papa,' Ursula Minor said. 'Except for the endless sleeping in winter.'

" 'A little variety would help,' Papa said, 'a little something extra to do.'

" 'Something more imaginative,' Ursula Mater said wistfully.

" 'What,' I proposed, 'about a spirited weekly seminar on the history of humankind?' "

"And its art, too?" my wife asked, trying to catch the waiter's good eye, which seemed to be floating about thoughtlessly.

"Of course," I said. "What do you take me for?"

"Wouldn't that have been hard, without the visuals?"

"I thought I would make drawings on the cave walls, a history of Western art on stone."

"What a splendid audience for your Eurocentricities," she said, fetchingly but with a certain languor.

"The point is that they liked the idea and we set aside Tuesday afternoons for our little salon."

"Tuesdays are very good for laundering and for seminars," she said.

"To interest them, I started drawing pictures of famous

paintings with a cave in them, like Giotto's Saint Francis de Assisi standing before his."

"Before his what?" she asked.

"Before his birds and bears came and stole his acorns, trying his sainthood," I said. Then I added graciously, "Have you ever seen the bubbles cheese makes under a blowtorch?"

She gave out a polite whale's yawn. "Those lucky bears," she said, "all that history delivered right to their door."

"And it was free," I said, "and loads of fun, and they were very grateful. But after two weeks, Ursula Mater took me aside.

" 'Look,' she said, 'no offense to you, but we've made a decision to leave here.'

"I was immediately sad for the loss for my friends, but then I grew frightened of my prospects, myself alone in the cave with no way to feed myself, and without means of finding my way back to—dare I say?—civilization. To wander in the mountains, to starve, to be eaten by dancing, frothing snakes!

" 'To go where?' I asked. 'Another mountain, another cave?'

" 'Back to the circus,' she said.

" 'To the old slavery and abuse, back to its routine and dreary monotony?' I asked, without irony, without anything but chagrin and the sense that my world had just darkened, shades darker than our cave at night—because even at night, the moonlight sometimes carpeted our entrance and coated the rough walls a cool silver.

"The strange thing, Ursula Mater said, was that they missed

dressing up—Ursula Major liked his straw boater and porkpie hat, his green bow tie and seersucker suit with the red sash, she liked her yellow apron and matching bonnet—Ursula Minor missed his baseball cap and catcher's mitt the size of a cherry pie. They all missed the crowds and the applause, the giant tent and the loud music. They also missed showing up the lions, who had really little to do by way of performance, theirs being the job of self-negation, of cowering and leaping through hoops, of being submissive, of showing how all their power could crumble at the crack of a whip.

"They even missed their old acts, she continued—the tight-wire, the piano solos, the teas with the midget and sometimes drunk Goldilocks—not to forget the applause they brought.

" 'There's that, the applause,' I said.

"Not to return to the old routines, not to the old slavery, not entirely: they had a plan."

"Which was?" she asked, her voice and the way she hovered over yet another martini showing no intense interest in getting an answer. The herrings, schools and all, had beaten a retreat, so now there was little of novelty left in the sky for me to bring to her attention—and from that diversion lead her back to my story.

What a failure, I thought, with a nonreflecting mirror for a head, with a head filled with odd tales of little compelling power. For all the art history lectures—with visuals—for all my pantomimes and stories and games, for all my telling them of human history, of philosophy from ancient times, when even blind men sat in little shaded groves and discussed their love for beauty, I could not even keep content the bears in their den.

"Where have I mislaid my life, dear?" I asked.

"I'm sure I don't know," she answered, with an olive between her teeth, like a little cannonball ready to be fired.

"It seems I have left it behind me somewhere," I said, looking about the empty garden, as if it had gone to another, less demanding table.

"Why don't you ask around?" she said. "Someone's bound to have found it."

The waiter appeared in his jodhpurs and rose ballet shoes; he was bent low, looking for wayward ants, his long belt trailing along the gravel.

"I think I'll order a dozen martinis," I said, "and see how many I can drink before they get warm."

"That's a wonderful idea," she said. "We can save the leftovers for breakfast tomorrow. Have them with the sardines."

"Better with salmon," I said, "raw, cold from the stream, and still quivering."

"You should know," she said respectfully.

And with that settled and my authority restored, I continued my story, disregarding my audience's indifference for the sake of its completion—for the selfish sake of my hearing again all that had happened.

"The ringmaster was not a stupid man, Ursula Mater said. Nor was the bear trainer. Not stupid, but their view was limited by all the years of the same bear acts performed with little variation the world over. It was the family's idea to add some new material to their show, which they would create, and blend with the known and traditional—the tightwire, the tea party, etc.

" 'Talking bears!' I shouted. 'That's what they will see and hear. Forget the acts, the routines, the stunts: talking bears!—it will make the circus billions and you won't have a say in anything you want to do.'

" 'Talking is not included,' she said, 'not part of the deal.'

" 'Your deal, not theirs,' I said. 'And even if they agree, when the word gets out, the scientists will come and put you in cages more horrible than you have ever known in the circus. And they will do things to you that no bear can imagine.'

"They had vowed, should their wishes not be met, to end their lives What would the circus have gained then?

" 'Kill yourselves?' Impossible, I thought. 'With what means would you be able to effect such a thing?' I asked smugly.

"She gave me a long bear look, suggestive of sympathy for me and pity for my blindness.

" 'With our imagination, of course,' she said.

" 'But why have it come to that?' I asked, in a chastened way—because I felt chastened, humbled by a bear—why, when they could stay here in their cave and live so pleasantly, live to see Ursula Minor have a family with a brood of cubs for them to fuss over in a grandparenty way?

" 'No,' she said. They had decided.

"Then I hit on a brilliant idea, I thought.

"'Why not create your new acts and perform them for me?' I suggested. Ursula Mater paused, excused herself, and went into conference with the others, returning to say that—with all respect to me—an audience of one was almost like none at all. Leaving apart the costumes and the music and the jealous lions.

"'And the applause,' I reminded.

"'There's that,' she said. 'Anyway, you would have grown bored watching us after a while, and then we'd all be in the same place but older.'

"I saw the wisdom in that, I said. But I was sad nevertheless.

"The strange thing was that I was happy in that cave. A fat candle or two for the night would have enlivened the atmosphere, but I had grown used to the dark and to the wispy sighs and meaty snores of the bears at sleep.

"We finally left, surviving many dull adventures along the way, many close escapes from bands of dancing snakes, but we eventually reached the outskirts of the town where the circus was quartered. I was the bears' emissary and delivered to the incredulous ringmaster the family's desires and terms for their return, to which he agreed before I brought him to their hiding place in a stand of trees behind a newly built shopping mall abutting a vast car-filled asphalt lot.

"We said our farewells. How far are the words of goodbye compared to our feelings of loss in leaving those we love, but never as far as when you say farewell to bears, their chocolate aroma already vanishing into the vanilla landscape of tires and cars and mall."

Now it was night and little strings of friendly lights encircled the garden walls, keeping the darkness on the poorer side of the street, so to speak. Soon it would be time for an early dinner, and afterward a little stroll for digestion's sake. Then to bed in one of the upper suites, facing the museum, where we would visit again in the morning after breakfast, when perhaps the sardines would at last appear.

We intended to eat lightly, as it was hot, even in the privileged enclave of the garden, where nothing of man or nature should have been allowed to discomfort us. What is the point of luxury, after all, if not to shield you from the irritations suffered by the many?

I ordered the salmon again, thinking one might emerge under the shelter of night, but this new waiter also shared his predecessor's principles in not negotiating what was not inscribed on the menu. I had asked again, thinking that just to say the word "salmon" might magically conjure us up a cool breeze drawn from my old bear cave, where so many of that fish had floundered about on the cold stone floor waiting to die.

We ate in silence, silently. All our conversation seemed spent. I had spent it. The dishes cleared, the waiter returned and asked me, "Coffee, cheese?"

"Coffee," I said.

"And the cheese?"

"She'll have the same," I said.

When he went away, she declared, "It's not much fun conversing with an unhappy mirror."

"Discontented mirror," I corrected.

"You might as well be a plate, because for the moment you reflect nothing, though I thought I saw a hint of me reflected there a half hour ago."

"Let's go to bed and dive right to sleep and strive for a better day tomorrow," I said flatly. "A day of fasting, a day without food or art, without conversation, even."

"And let's purge all thoughts, as well, let's wash clean the slate," she said. "Not even talk," she prescribed. "Mute, silent, empty, then let's start afresh, a bright mirror and a sharp slice of cheese," she added, as we rose in the elevator.

"*Da cord,*" I said, holding her to me once we slid into bed. We kissed on the cheeks and held hands, like the old friends, after all the years, we had become.

"*Bone nooey,*" she said, letting out a dainty sigh into her pillow.

Sometime in the night, I woke and went up to the window and faced the museum, where whole lives were resting on the walls, paintings, any one of which I would have gladly exchanged years of my life to have painted. Five years for Goya's dog staring, with all the might of his dog's soul, into space, seeing in the air what invisible presences no humans have the eyes to see.

Ten years I'd give—fifteen, even—for Velázquez's *Las*

Meninas, where in a darkened room a cave of royals, king and queen, are framed in a distant mirror, and a princess and her ladies-in-waiting, dwarfs and a sturdy dog sit for their portrait, the artist viewing them in a mirror and watching himself in another mirror painting them. Velázquez had conceived the world as an ungraspable reflection of mirrors, endlessly reflecting and refracting analogies back and forth through time and place. I was sure that eventually, one day in eternity, I would look at the painting and see myself and my darling bears cavorting in a mountain stream at the canvas edge.

I returned to bed, where, as elsewhere, nothing of mine had ever flowered, except my dreams. And soon I slept and soon I dreamed.

My bears were home, back in the circus again, performing acts of their own invention. Befitting the true artists they had become, their heads were mirrors, but unlike mine, their mirrors reflected everything about them, and absorbed everything about them, the whole giant red tent and the world beneath it, lions, seals, elephants, the large wheels of cheese being rolled on their side by chimps with hats topped with salmons smoking cigars. Reflected, even, a troupe, all in plaid bow ties, of dancing green snakes from our old mountains—their mouths no longer frothing—dancing their elastic skinny dance.

The audience shone in their mirrors, too: children with eyes open wider than the sky at night; adults healthy and dying indifferent to their fate; lovers pausing in their lust;

moms and dads sweating gladly in their Sunday best, staring enviously at the family of happy bears, happy as families never are. And I was there, caught in their mirrors as well. Me, alone, at night, in the shadow of a museum the size of a mountain, in a moonlit cave in a graveled garden, at a table with a red umbrella, at a table humming with eyes.

Self Portrait with Icebergs

They were speaking the language of young gulls and beardless seals, the language of childless ice splintering in the Arctic sun. But I understood them, having myself spoken those same languages long ago, when once I drifted, alone, on ice floes under frozen skies. They did not notice me when I entered the apartment, so engrossed were they, those two, musing on maps and charts, searching sea routes to secret islands shrouded by the massive cries of birds.

Finally, turning from her ruminations, she asked me, "What are more beautiful, words or objects?"

"You are more beautiful," I said, trying not to look at her directly, lest she see what a fool I was. More beautiful now that the room was bare, stripped of distracting furniture, except for a mattress on the floor and a laptop sizzling on a wooden table.

Lighting a cigarette as if he were in a gale and letting my flattery pass, her lover turned to me. "And what is more wonderful, adventure or death?"

"Words," I said, with a wise man's expression, meant to assure him I was beyond the concerns of the flesh and lived only in the sphere of thought—where thoughts of her never set foot. In truth, I thought of them both often, living in the apartment above theirs and facing the same tame park, which for me was all the green world I needed, nature being my old enemy. Though, for them, the park always spoke of exciting vistas to come, trees meant forests and jungles, the lightest dust of snow a tundra.

"Can you shiver a timber? Or hoist a tankard? Or coil a line? Or do any of those things seamen are called to do?" she asked, loading an old leather suitcase with cartons of cigarettes.

"Of course," I said, "and I can set a sail and hitch a sextant to the pole star; I can raise ship with an 'avast' and an 'ahoy,' I can make whales thrill to my song." I could, but for the moment I so much more preferred to whistle for a taxi as it rushed down Avenue A or hitch my laundry bag over my shoulder and amble to the Laundromat with its row of exciting, spinning machines.

"You are just the man to sail with us," they whispered in chorus.

Now I finally understood why the maps and charts and

why a schooner was moored across the street, in the middle of Tompkins Square Park, the bare elm trees bending in ice, the snow climbing the ship's gunwales, her running lights smeared with frost, the whole of her shivering out there in the wintry cold where only yesterday it was spring.

"Perhaps," I said, "but not tonight or tomorrow or any other day or night or century to come. In any case, for what port are you bound?

"To none but to the ends of the earth, to the end of words," she said.

"To their transmutation," he added sweetly, "to the truths behind their veils."

"For that," I said, "we need only stay here, in our apartments, where we can cast spells upon ourselves and conjure up all sorts of beguiling enchantments."

"All enchantments," he said, adjusting his watch cap, "wait at the border of the unknown, where imagination has never ventured."

"That is where death is," I said, in a voice from long ago, the voice of that man waiting to die on the ice.

They suddenly took each other's hands, like babes braving the dull woods of the commonplace, like a dark brother and pale sister who had lived in their safe castle too long and who had fed their imaginations only with books and the alimentation of the Internet and who craved, against all precaution, experience of the world outside their barred windows.

Suddenly she turned to me, her smile a command. "Lie

down," she said, pointing to the mattress on the bare wooden floor, "lie down and look up."

Which of course I did, gladly, for her, seeing above me on the ceiling the Southern Hemisphere, with all its wondrous constellations and mysterious arrangements of stars, whose drifting patterns I had puzzled over long ago, in the frozen nights, when I had nothing to read but the sky.

"We know that heaven by heart," he said, pocketing a small compass, "and all the safe sea roads beneath, as well."

"So we are at ease in the matter of this voyage," she said, "as we have memorized all the lanes of our watery fate and go to meet it unafraid."

"And so now," he said, "there is nothing left for us but to voyage to where contraries finally meet and burst into dreams."

"Yes, that mission also bewitched me once, when I was young like you," I said. "When I thought my invulnerable ship could override seas taller than destiny and ice mountains grander than hope."

"Why not revive," they said, "the dreams of your youth, making them the life of the moment?"

It was a terrifying idea, the revival of my youth, the revival also of my terrors, my ship splintered, my shipmates drowned in the freezing rivers of the ocean, myself struck from a mast, a bobbing chip riding on an ice plate in the sea.

I was about to tell them the story of that voyage, a cautionary tale to keep them safely at home, to keep their young hair from turning insanely white, to keep their perfect hearts from crumbling in fear. But I was halted by the rumbling and grinding noise coming from the refrigerator, a noise that kept growing until the door burst open, exploding hundreds of ice cubes across the floor. Even after she ran to yank the plug from its socket, the ice kept flowing out from the fridge, streaming across the room, spreading and steadily mounting in jagged piles and perfect pyramids.

"It will stop eventually, I suppose," she said, kicking away the little mountain rising at her feet.

"Just never mind," he added, "we won't be here much longer anyway."

"Leaving soon?" I asked, alarmed at the prospect of their departure and sad to be left behind on a street, in a house, where they will have vanished like twin breezes. I would no longer meet them at the café on Tenth Street and First Avenue, where Valentina, the waitress, who was born among the coffee sacks and who dreamed of rafting the Amazon, encouraged us to read Plato as a tonic for the blood and a catalyst for prophetic dreams.

"Tonight," she answered, as if the world were compressed into that word.

"In an hour or so, when the tide turns," he amplified earnestly.

Hadn't the tide turned long ago? And had it not taken my youth and all its furniture with it out to sea, which now waited to carry me away and drown me in its mad black depths? For that reason I never left home, never unhooked the anchor chained to my leg, lest a wind of adventure take me from my mooring and drive me out again into the dangerous watery world, which, finally, is most of the world.

Now the ice cubes were mounting to my ankles, chilling me. I thought of returning to my apartment, where a plant or two awaited rain from my watering can, where my cat, Nicolino, his whiskers at military attention, stood guard at my door. And then, of course, there were the comforting books in piles mounting to the ceiling, little walkways dividing the hills of volumes. Books, after all, are safer than persons, safer than banks, safer than marriage, safer than ships and boats and ice floes, safer than walls of loneliness.

"Before we leave, would you like an orange?" she asked, cupping one in her hand like a golden globe of the world.

How wonderful, that orange, illuminating the gray room and the white ice with its warm, sunny glow.

"Or maybe you would prefer this?" he said, holding out a pineapple, which bathed the room in a dreamy tropical heat.

Soothing, that warm glow and soft heat of sunny places, where parrots screech and hummingbirds hum above golden sands and green seas, where the tortoise reckons the sky his brother, where man sleeps away his days in the rainy season and wakes to make love in the burning summer.

Do you want ease and negligence or a life unexplored? That was what those two lovebirds were asking me with their offerings, with their maps and charts, fruits and ice cubes. Will you join us, they were asking, join us on a voyage to the Antarctic—for that was where they were bound—where the cold, with its icy splinters, will break open your dead heart like a casket on Judgment Day, leading you to a life yet unimagined, where books are just matchsticks to light a passionate fire?

"Look," I said, "consider how a ship fares in the plunge of even the calmest sea; consider how the whole of your voyage is but an inch in the day of time, where time is the sea on which we travel—now consider how our ship would fare in the plunging seas of wild time and icebergs."

"Sure," she said, putting on her red sealskin boots and sable hood, "who doesn't know that?"

"Know what?" I asked.

"That not everyone likes to travel, even on a steel train on a flat plate without clouds."

"You might want to know who else is coming aboard with us," he said, stuffing tea bags into his coat, "because not everyone alive was invited, in case you may have thought otherwise."

He produced a sheet with the names—some just indicated with an X—of the crew. I recognized among them Tony, who lived down the street and greeted everyone who passed with a complicated salute, whose meaning, he one day confided to us, would be revealed to him by an angel who lived far away in an ice cave. There also was Alonzo, the pizza deliveryman, who used his tips to feed the pigeons out there in the park—where the ice was now weighing down the trees and snapping off the branches—because they were the souls of uncles lost in the snows of the Andes. Valentina, the waitress from the café, had signed on, too. She and her Plato, I was sure, would light the black nights.

"I'm impressed," I said, "by the purity and philosophical nature of your crew, though there is not a sailor among them."

"Well, they are all questers," he said, "believers in the phantoms of words," he added, as his watch cap gleamed with stars, the smoke from his cigarette circling them like little winter clouds.

"Theirs is an inquiry into rumors and lost causes, you might say, if you were disposed to saying such things," she said, winding a giant red scarf about her neck.

"Once," I said, "I lived on an ice cake in Antarctica—for weeks, in a hut I cobbled from my wrecked ship's planks and beams. I lived there, in the cold and wet, under a lead sky, whose leaden sheets pressed me down to the waterline, so that I existed on the horizontal, squeezed between sky and ice. Sometimes seals came up to poke their noses at me and to sing—more beautiful music than I had ever heard in a church, wonderful hymns to God they were, and I was often the soloist in their choir—accompanied often by the altos of gulls. Heavenly days of hell, where death was more welcome than life."

She took my hand, then the other hand, and regarded me for some moments. "You will need gloves," she said. "We have learned that above all else, warm gloves are the key to a voyage of this nature." I felt, warmer than any gloves, the cool heat of her hands.

"Your tale has many vivid qualities," he said, donning his third sweater, "but none so compelling as to change our minds."

"Or our hearts," she added.

The ice cubes had now climbed the walls and lathered the ceiling, leaving naked only the large windows to the park. A glistening igloo of ice the room had become—the two of them sat on a block of ice, a seal-oil lamp for warmth, their eyes filled with light, which flowed through the moonlit window. How could I stay behind, when they unceremoniously could transform nature with their desire and, with the power of imagination and words, transform rooms into igloos, stay-at-homes into adventurers—transform me?

Theirs was a magic without tricks. Their magic—like their youth—defied gravity, darkness, and bad weather. Which was the present condition—the deep night bloomed outside the snow-lashed window. Seagulls and cormorants, silvered in the moon, swarmed about the park, fluttering about the lampposts like trembling sheets. A polar bear with her two cubs lumbered by the ship without a parting glance. Perched high atop a flagpole, a white penguin contemplated the scene.

Yellow lights in the portholes, red lanterns fore and aft, the running lights a string of cold pearls, the rigging alive with small pineapple bulbs interspersed with orange globes—the ship glowed like a burning fruit encased in ice.

"You can see," he said, in a most affectionate way, waving his baby harpoon like a magician's wand over the glowing icy scene out the window, "how things are with us now, how oxymoron may be created in the service of splitting the dialectic, how, finally, desire overmasters all trepidation—yours and ours."

There was no more to say, no more hesitation. In a flash I was in my apartment and gathering up my cat, who joined me without a thought or a question and who seemed pleased by our impending departure. Even my old books appeared glad to have me go and to be left, with the plants, to ripen by themselves for a while. Odd, how no one misses you when you are brave.

And then we were downstairs at the entrance where the two were waiting with their gear—suddenly a silvery skiff appeared and glided us to the ship.

Once on board, I felt the familiar dread of the unknown world return to me, and I turned to look up at my apartment window, still glowing in the golden lights I had forgotten to switch off. There was still time to go back, all I had to do was jump across the islands of ice forming about the ship, and there I would be, home and safe again. The crew, with Nicolino at their side, stood looking at me expectantly, little chunks of ice fastening like barnacles to their shivering coats. It would obviously take me some months to make this crew seaworthy.

"Well," he said, taking out his old pocket watch, "shall we get started?"

"Yes," she said, turning to me, "let's sail."

"Weigh anchor," I said, without another thought but of the road ahead.

And off we went, sailing out of the park and coursing directly down Avenue B, passing along the way the library and the schoolhouse, the newsstand and the theater, passing all our known life, as the snowy wind filled our sails and drove us down the East River and through the Narrows, speeding us beyond the Statue of Liberty and out to the open sea.

Self Portrait with Beach

The beach, the sea, the blue umbrellas. A sail. Then another, like a long arm climbing the horizon. She stretched out on a blanket beside me in the dreadful hot sand. A sheet of gulls wheeling and diving, a form emerging from under the flat sea. Flat, feverless, an ocean too exhausted to make waves, an ocean that had seen too much travel. I was thinking this when she asked, "Is the body the house for the soul or are body and soul one and inseparable?" She slipped off her bikini top, exposing her breasts to the sky, to the gaze of the sea.

"Your body is my soul," I said.

She laughed, in a friendly way, as if to assure me that in spite of what seemed my exaggeration, she was pleased.

"Poor you," she said finally, "stuck with a soul bound for decay."

"Nothing of you will decay," I said, "not as long as I'm alive." And in love, I wanted to add, for the truth of it. But certain truths are better left at home, under a pillow, nesting among the feathers.

The beach was filling up with little clusters of families staking their territory with umbrellas and chairs. Young couples, hungry to burn their bodies, marked their separate terrain, spreading mats and towels under the raw sun.

Out of nowhere a young man in white cap, white jacket, and creamy pants appeared, crooning the virtues of his home-made beverages, kept in a white box he shouldered. He was a white thing itself come from out of the blue, where most thoughts and fictions reside.

"Where did you come from?" I asked, having not seen him in our view before he materialized in whiteness and smiles.

"Out there," he said, nodding to the ocean. "A cold beverage?" he asked. Cold. Cold like love gone cold, I was sure he added, but knew he had not.

"Maybe later," I said. "Try us again later when it gets really hot."

We should buy now, he said, because his was a special home-brewed drink—it had unique powers.

"Do you have any to make one young again?" I asked, feeling ancient, like a sea who has washed up on too many shores.

"Yes, and beautiful, as well," he replied. "I have many sorts of flavors and specialties. This one, for example," he said, drawing a small bottle from his jacket pocket, "is to keep your woman faithful."

"Oh! Fidelity," she said. "I'm surprised it hasn't already exploded in your pocket," she added.

"This one never explodes," he said. "The body explodes before this does." He had a wonderful grin, white like his hair.

"I don't require the fidelity drink," she said, looking at me.

"But I would like the youth-restorative flavor," I said. "Give me three, if you have them."

"I'm all out," he said, rummaging through his box. "It's an all-time favorite."

"Come back when you have more," she said. "We'll be here all day, we'll wait here for years."

"Of course, I would do the same," he said, giving her a sweet, devouring look that made me jealous. I could see her blush, even through the blanching sunlight. Another smile, wider than the first, then he sauntered away, singing all the while the praise of his magical beverages.

"You only love me because you find me beautiful," she said, "and so when that's gone, I'm gone, too. Right?"

"Of course not," I said, half lying.

"And if I were a real soulless bitch, you'd still love me because I was beautiful. Right?"

"Let's not go into metaphysics," I said as if I had meant it.

Her long smooth legs, her strong feet, bronzed, like the rest of her, by the sun. Her beauty that I loved and wanted always to stay the same, through aging and death, through at least the next few years. I was superficial about wanting her to remain young forever—never more than her twenty-eight perfect years, never less than perfect.

Superficial in other ways as well, she would say—had said. We can find beauty everywhere, I once proclaimed, and in everything, even in the decay of roses and in the corpses of dead seagulls on the beach, in the scars on otherwise smooth flesh, but there is no beauty like the body of any creature in its perfect, healthy form. A perfect body shields all the blemishes and corruptions of the soul, makes them irrelevant to our regard, I once—late at night in bed, in an after-love drowse— had announced to her, to my regret.

A single-engine plane, trailed by a banner selling a fleet of desires, flew sleepily by, the propeller's old-fashioned hum bringing me back to my childhood on the beach, to my mother, bringing me to her tender smile under a wide yellow hat that defied the sun. Her breasts were full then and beautiful with the fullness of youth not yet overripened. The bodies we feast upon as children dominate the future landscape of our desire, imprinting forever all our dreams of beauty—and of unsightliness.

The sun was now on her thighs, spread discreetly, like temple gates in Arcadia. I had sketched her while she slept that morning, exhausting five large sheets of good paper before I realized—once again—how she always eluded me. I had turned her legs into the pillars of Hercules, her breasts into small bread loaves, the rest of her I had converted into a birch tree without branches.

Courbet would have painted her richly, ripe thighs open to creating the world, if he had not viewed her—as he did women—as a metaphor. Renoir would have made her stupidly fleshy, a bourgeois bred on pastries, though she was lean like boundaries on a map. Gauguin would have transformed her into a child of the jungle, when she was nothing of nature except for her desires.

I myself had failed at it completely, as I had so many other things in life. My paintings rendering just the bare image of her but not the paradigms of her in my heart. The canvas was often left bare, with a few lines here and there to consecrate the quixotic memory of my ambition. More than any photograph, those lines etched her image in my mind, gathered up her scent, her voice, her twisted hairpins on the pillow. Of course, these are fancy words to cover my inability to draw a line that hinted at her soul, her true immortal form.

"I had a dry period after you left the last time," she said, turning on her stomach.

"Did it last long?" I asked, fearful of knowing about her life without me. Wanting never to leave her, always leaving her and taking my chances that she would be there when I returned. And fearful, too, of her answer, I began studying the curve of her breasts as if for the first time, with the wonder of the first time.

"Until you returned," she said, like the friendly breeze that had come from the sea. She smiled and reached her hand out to mine, which was not far away, waiting, as it were, for hers.

Three teenagers sauntered by, loving themselves in a fidgety, insecure way, amazed by the newly found power of their bodies to unhinge reason and jolt planets from their orbits. They gave us a passing glance and, seeing nothing but age, did not see us.

She rose on her elbows, trailing my field of vision. The two of us following them until they were no longer significant in our view.

"How long do you think I have?" she asked. "Staying passable, I mean."

"Aphrodite lives forever," I said.

"How long is that?" she asked.

"Five years for others, a hundred for me."

"Five years?" she said. "Five minutes, then. Five waves of the hand."

"Even when the young men stop looking," I said consolingly, "others will take their place, the older ones."

The vendor returned promoting his drinks, walking back and forth, and every once in a while he would give her a long look, taking her in with evident, unaffected joy. How wonderful that one can give so much pleasure to another, without effort, merely by being, I thought. But not without feeling jealous that the young man's gaze, like a magnet, had drawn some part of her youth, her beauty, into himself, leaving less of her for me. The voyeur is always a thief. I'm a prince of such thieves.

"Sometimes when you were gone I thought of sleeping around. Although 'around' sounds too vast a territory for a girl to cover." She laughed. I did, too, but mirthlessly.

Some clouds appeared out of the blue. Giant, swollen gray bags they were, like frisky blimps looking for a port. I would have loved to be with them—away from all jealousy—floating up there, sailing from harbor to harbor.

"Did you?" I asked, dreading her answer.

"What harm would it have done, after all, what would it have mattered once I'm in the grave?"

"I thought you intended to be cremated," I said, trying to lighten the clouds.

"What comfort to my ashes, then?" she asked, shaking sand from her hair.

"'Ashes they shall become, but ashes in love.' Do you know that poem of Quevedo's?"

"You always quote it," she said. "I should know it by heart now. Is that how you love me, like an ash?"

"Always a glowing one," I said. "Glowing for you," I added for good measure, overflowing the cup. The three teenagers who had passed by earlier passed by again, but now they were middle-aged, with soft bellies and drooping chins, with children who had grown away, with husbands gone to younger women or gone to the grave. I could see that in them, their disappointments buried beneath their tans.

"I'm baked and I'm thirsty," she said, just as the vendor cast his handsome shadow over us. A strange shadow, considering that the sun, in some tricky maneuver, had darkened its complexion.

"I'm brewing up a new batch of drinks," he said. "Come up to the canteen for a fresh cup or two."

"The good stuff?" I asked. "The stuff of dreams?"

He smiled, like a flash of lightning. He smiled at her.

When we arrived at the canteen, we saw a long line back down to the shore. Hundreds of people, some holding their huge beach umbrellas over their heads, were waiting, silently, for the canteen doors to open. We had no desire to wait and were about to leave when he called out to us from the veranda.

"No, no, come here," he said, waving aside those at the front of the line to make way for us.

He sat us down at a wooden table under a thatched roof. He told us we would not have to wait long for his marvelous concoction to be ready, bringing us in, meanwhile, a pitcher of ice water and a bowl of olives. That was a strange combination, I said, water and olives. It was his canteen, he said, he could bring us anything we wanted. Even music, if we were lonely for music.

Lonely for music, what a notion, I thought. But I suddenly realized that I was lonely for a music that would take me from the beach and its heat, for a music that would suit the mood of longing, as I was then feeling, to have back my life from the start, when I was young enough to believe I would never grow old, would never die. As if on cue, two birds began singing. I could see their still forms lurking above us in the straw roof, the birds singing of desire and love, of love eternal, of love beyond the bodily frame, beyond the cells as they ecstatically crashed into blindness, silence, and death.

"How odd," she said, "birds singing in German."

"Yes," I said. "More so that they have human voices."

"I overlooked that nuance," she said.

"*Tristan und Isolde*," we said simultaneously. Then she added, "No, wrong. *Ariadne auf Naxos*."

"It's the same thing," I said, "passion, death, funeral pyres, love, besotted smoke ascending to the gods."

The singing ceased, voices rose from outside the veranda. The line had grown even longer, extending far down and along the shore, which had turned a squalid gray, like the gray sky and sea. There was grumbling in the line and some pressed themselves against the canteen walls as if to break them down. No one was young.

"Look," he said, "look at the love birds." He held up a pair of golden metal nightingales by their metal tails. "I have musical chips for every mood, even Puccini, if you prefer the sweetness."

"Oh!" she said. "Mechanical birds with chips for every mood."

I hated the deflation in her voice. She was still young and not steadied for disappointments.

"They are not expensive," he said. "I could let you have them for a price." He smiled at me in a reassuring way as he would to her uncle, then at her. "For a kiss," he said.

"I'd rather have the drinks," she said in a polite way that carried other meanings.

"Which you both shall have," he said, covering her rebuke with a face of smiles.

"And the others waiting out there?" I asked.

"They have had their share many times," he said, "while you have had none." Suddenly his voice was that of an older man's and not that of the youth who earlier had paraded the beach shouldering his wares. He looked older, his skin gone dry, his body stooped over our table.

"I don't think we want your drink," she said, turning to me as she spoke. "Do we?"

"I don't know," I said lightly. "I wouldn't mind trying the youth restorative. What harm could it do?"

She gave me a long look, as if to say, Why waste time on this charlatan? Why give away a moment of life that is not a moment spent together, when every second in this world steals us away from each other? And finally, and perhaps to the core of it all, Why let him flirt with me?

"What harm?" I repeated lamely, feeling, indeed, that in wanting, now more than ever, his magic drink, I had gone lame, at least in her eyes if not in mine.

"Stay," she said. "I'll take a walk along the beach and find you back at our umbrella."

The sky was darkening in an unfriendly way. I wanted to point that out to her, as if the weather were my concern, when what I really wanted to say was, Don't leave. Don't take that walk without me, don't shut down your heart from me for even a second, but then I thought of how wonderful being young again would be and I said, "I won't be long."

I watched her leave—without a kiss—watched her walk away slowly, so that by the time he had brought me my drink, she was far away, growing smaller, a diminishing dot against the blustery sky.

I was back in my beach chair but no longer needed the umbrella, as the sun was walled in by the darkest clouds. I kept the umbrella open so that she might better see me in the distance and also because as the beach began to empty, slowly at first and then at a faster pace, the rain drizzled down from the clouds. It would take a half hour or so, he said, before I would feel the effects of the drink, and then maybe an hour or two longer before the results were visible. Little hints of change at first, such as an improvement in my hearing and sight, or a feeling of tightness of the skin under my chin, which had begun its slide with gravity. And then, if all went well, in a matter of a few more hours I would be back to my optimum moment of health and youth, back to the golden age of twenty-eight, give or take a year or two.

The sea was rising and gulls were screaming at the waves. The swimmers had long ago returned to shore. The sea was empty, the beach emptier. Not a chair, not an umbrella, not a person in sight. I looked and looked in the direction of where I had last seen her walk and saw nothing but darkening space in retreat. Then the rain began in earnest, drowning the sea and the beach and flooding the canteen, which had already locked its doors and fastened the shutters, looking long ago abandoned. I was the only soul on the beach, the only soul on earth. I should pick myself up, I thought, and leave the beach, but I could not, did not wish to move, or change my place for any place in the world, waiting, under an umbrella in a deluge, as I was, for the return of my youth.

The Park in Winter

"Do you think about that much?" she asked, setting down her glass.

"The instant I'm under the covers," I said. "The instant I shut my eyes."

I didn't tell her the other part, where I dream my body is driven away and lugged to a funeral parlor, where they gut my internal organs like so much glop from a melon, and where they drain my blood and shoot chemicals into my dry veins to keep me from stinking up the visitors, should any come to see me, my cheeks rouged and me dandified, in the open casket.

"You're still too young for such morbid thoughts," she said.

"No one is too young, darling. 'Thou hast neither youth nor age, but, as it were, an after-dinner's sleep dreaming on both.' That's Shakespeare, you know."

She gave me a long look, not too withering.

It was still snowing out the window and, of course, snowing in the city beyond. Snow whirling about the leafless trees in the icy park. So beautiful out there as long as you were in the warm inside. Her hands were still cold from our walk in the park, she said. I reached over to warm them. But she drew back.

"The quote's fine, but you needn't have patronized me with the attribution."

"A bad habit I picked up from Henry," I said. "Forgive me."

"Oh! Blaming the dead," she said with a little laugh.

"Don't you remember how Henry'd say things like '*pardonnez-moi*' or '*bonjour*' and then add, 'That's French, you know'?"

"But he was joking. You weren't," she said.

We could have gone back and forth on this matter for the night, so finally I said, "I suppose so." A small admission to prevent larger battles and perhaps greater defeats. I turned to look for the waiter, who had again vanished from the room after bringing our drinks. I shrugged, as if to say to her, Well, I've done what I can do, but I can't just make him appear.

Just then she smiled and made a little salute in the air, producing, on the instant, our missing waiter. A figure of speech, of course, as he was never ours. To whom did he belong? To what woman or man, to what marmalade cat waiting at home?

"Another round?" he asked her with a smile.

"First one, and then another, and then, who knows?" she said.

He smiled again. He liked her. Most times I did, too.

What kind of waiter are you, I wanted to ask in a joking way, when you are always disappearing? Shouldn't a waiter wait? Stay in one place, I mean, until called for. But then he might have said, I'm a server, not a waiter. Or something clever like that. And who knows where that exchange would lead us, finally.

We had been all morning, she and I, at the Met, just across the street, and had taken our lunch in late afternoon at the same hotel where we were staying and in whose clubby bar we were now having our evening drinks. Our past three days were spent ferrying happily from hotel to museum, from bar to bed. We had enjoyed ourselves. We were at an age when enjoying ourselves was important; it having taken most of our youth to learn to distill the gold from the ore, to relish each day as a gift for the day only. Not that you ever learn that completely, only a few geniuses for living know that, and they are born with the talent.

Most of us muddle along until it is too late to apply what we've learned about living to what days remain of our life. Give me back the years, we cry, hurtling to the other side, where time vanishes into dark space. Portentous, she says of me, and always looking into gloomy rooms and seeing whole tragedies in the dusty corners. She's right, I suppose. Sometimes an apple is just an apple and not the image of the Fall. Sometimes a dark room is just a dark room and not the mirror of our solitary place in hell, where we are all alone, far from

God, and know we deserve to be. Better hell than extinction, in any case.

She looked out of the window and at the whirling snow driving into the lumbering Fifth Ave buses, into the sluggish taxis, into the faces of young couples laughing in their benighted happiness. The snow, themselves, their youth, their laughter, their forever. My jealousy, of course, not to be out there among them, owning the world with them in the piling snow.

Then she turned to me and very sweetly said, "I suppose you still miss Henry."

"All the time, don't you?"

"Not the way you do, I think."

"Which way is that?"

"Excessively, the way you miss everything you miss. That's just an observation," she said, "not a criticism."

"I'm grateful for the distinction," I said.

Wonderful, all this banter, setting us up for battles in the bed waiting for us in a warm room six stories above our heads. Tension is the best aphrodisiac, short of anger—unless you are in love, when the world winnows down to a bed in a room without clocks, and the simple brush of arm against arm arouses you. We were still youngish, with time left for erotic play. We were, after all, still burning, while many of our friends were now just ashes.

Of any period in history, I asked Henry, where would he want to be?

"Oh! I'm happy enough here," he said, "with the friends."

He would have been most happy, I always thought, in an Elizabethan inn, roasting luxuriously before the fireplace, while the winter outside froze stones in the fields and kine in their huddle. And talking, talking, talking, expanding the air with Elizabethan words in a room filled with Elizabethan friends. In whatever climate, time, or place, friends made him happy. Beautiful ones. "With brains," he'd add.

There were many such who came to visit and he hoped would stay the night. Artists who wanted him to visit their studios or write a praising line about their work, or writers or poets all liking to be near him, he who was believed to have the power to anoint the young and raise them to fame. I once left him alone after dinner with a poet of twenty, fresh and golden like a young lion first come down from the mountains to consider the sea. Henry phoned me in the morning to say the poet had left not long after I had.

"He kissed me on the cheek," he said, "like a nephew leaving me for his date."

I was sorry, I told him, for his disappointment. Well, of course, there was that, he said, but it was all compensated for by the little talk they had at the door about Byron and his circle.

"I had no idea young people read Byron anymore," I said. Actually, I didn't know anyone who now did, but it's always meanly satisfying to blame the young for the darkening of the culture.

"Well, it wasn't the poetry, you see. He was smitten by Byron's life, by how Byron and some of his friends heaped Shelley's corpse on a stack of burning wood and burned most of him away."

"That must have been romantic for you, all that talk of cremation."

"He was sweet, I must say. When there is no sex, sweetness counts. He offered to do the same for me, when the time came; he and his young poet friends, take me to a beach at dawn and burn me down to ashes."

"Of course, there's the unpoetical matter of gathering the firewood and getting the permits," I told him. "Not that they would ever get them."

"It was the thought," he said, "the sweet thought, that mattered."

"Of course," I said, "I was only joking." I was.

"Just because a person doesn't want to sleep with you doesn't mean he doesn't love you," Henry said.

"There's no mystery there," I said.

"The mystery to me," he said, "is why we are attracted to what we're attracted to."

That was a mystery we talked about a long time, until we finally agreed that, as with all attempts to define beauty, we would get nowhere.

Finally, Henry said, "Let's face it, all beauty is youth, all youth is beauty."

"How silly," I said. "And, of course, utterly untrue. A human, like a work of art, increases in desirability over time," I said. Aura counts in life as in art. Only time and experience generate the aura that gives a person his or her distinctive desirability. The people you've slept with and have loved, for example; how much and how deeply you've read, by what means you have earned your money, the kindnesses you've shown in life. All that and more create a person's aura, which is to say his or her attractiveness or unattractiveness.

"Of course, you don't really believe that," Henry said. He was fingering an old Roman coin with the head of young Antinous, beloved of Emperor Hadrian. Henry loved that coin and its history and asked to be buried with it in his hand. Which, finally, he wasn't, as his body, at the end, went naked into the crematorium.

"Well, I believe it to some degree, but not by much," I confessed. "Or if I did, it wouldn't affect my idea of who I'd want to sleep with."

"So, finally, you're as limited as I am. Beauty is youth and youth, beauty—just as I've always said."

"And then, with those words, he died," she said, wanting to cut me off and return the night to her. I had, as some people say, no problem with that.

"Not die just then, in midthought, so to speak, but in due course," I said. Whatever that meant, "in due course." A sailing term, perhaps, as in "to keep on due course"? Or meaning something that will happen in the inevitable course of time. How many such expressions had I used in my life without knowing their exact meaning or source?

How much time is due us, anyway—in the sense that time is obliged to give itself to us? Who, in any case, would want to oblige time to empty out its pockets and leave us without a penny's worth of itself? To run out of money, to run out of time. All in due course, of course.

"Do you want to go up?" I asked. "It's snowing too hard to go out again, even if we wanted to."

She looked about, distractedly, I thought.

"Are you distracted?"

"Not at all, just looking for the waiter."

"Again?"

"Sure."

"Are you flirting with him?" I asked stupidly. Because what would I have done had she said yes? Stop flirting with him then, I could have said. As simple as to ask her to stop tapping her fingernail against her now-empty glass. But there were ramifications to the first question that would not have applied to the second.

"I don't think so," she said.

"Oh! It's never easy with men and women," I said, with a certain aplomb, a certain world-weary, enlightened resignation, a certain distracted charm—assuring her that my observation did not apply to the moment at hand, to her, but was of a more cosmic and Olympian nature. Aggression in the guise of a truism, Henry might have said. Correctly.

Suddenly a gaggle of couples rushed into the room. Laughing and brushing off the snow from their coats and seizing the empty banquettes. When the waiter finally appeared, he bypassed the newcomers and came directly over to us. I wondered what it was she may have seen or imagined she had seen in him. I have never been able to understand what a woman finds attractive in a man, never. Some man whom I supposed handsome and irresistible to a woman just leaves her cold; while some man I consider plain—just okay in the looks department—sends her spinning.

I took the waiter in, then, to imagine what she—what a woman—might fancy in him. He was very tall and very thin. His black hair was slicked back thirties-style. Hawk's beak on a narrow face. Rimless glasses. Tux with hand-drawn bow tie. I could have taken him for one of the hotel guests just come from some formal affair, a benefit dinner, perhaps, one of the dozen elegant ones given every night in the city. He was a grown man in his early thirties, maybe a little too old for his job, unless he was a true failure, for which there is no age minimum or limit. Some women like collapsed men, whose failure shines handsomely. I was stretching the point, of course. She may have just liked his indifference to his job or to her or she might have fancied his beak or that he frequently had disappeared into another room beyond the bar, perhaps to a magical sphere all his own.

Some people at the other tables called out to him but he did not even turn about to acknowledge or to mollify them.

"Another, again?" he said, speaking directly to her. "Or should I bring you a few dozen rounds for the table?"

"Is it still snowing?" she asked him. "I hate looking over my shoulder to see."

"Why don't the two of you go out and have a look?" I said matter-of-factly. I had long worked on that neutral, ironic tone, fashioning it into a kind of armor against a hurtful world.

He turned to me with a big smile full of chalky teeth. "Why don't you come out with me and see?"

Long ago, I went to India alone. It's sad to go to India alone. Much sadder than going to other places alone, like Rome, say, where, when eating alone at a table in a street of tables packed with voluble friends and family and lovers and stray cats, a deep self-pity for being the loneliest and the only lonely person in the world overtakes you. It would be different, you think, had you had someone with you, a lover—or at least a friend—or a dog to sit agreeably by your leg to share the evening and distract you, for the while, distract you from feeling yourself the loneliest person in the world. In Rome, defeating loneliness is a matter of peopling the table.

But in India, you know, in truth, that you are finally alone, lonely like a snowflake atop an ocean wave; that for all the people milling about you, there is no one in the whole and busy earth but you, all the others being props—illusions—to populate the scene.

I stayed healthy in India, while many tourists about me were falling like gassed flies into the soup. I drank the tap water and ate the uncooked vegetables and still I went about the day at full steam, while others at my hotel, more cautious than I, had turned green, dysentery being the least of their feverish worries. I went in full health to Benares, seeking what I knew I would see there, so I was not surprised by the partially cremated human bodies drifting in the river, not surprised by the burning and stinking riverbank and hungry dogs with charred human bones in their teeth. I had come exactly to see all that, to humble myself in the face of Death. But I had not expected the loneliness that had set in and that had made Death seem not too unwelcome a someday visitor. Not that I was brave or had wanted oblivion; extinction, however, is more finite than loneliness, which lasts beyond death.

That was a funny thing, I thought, when I thought it then, there, in India, on the slippery, ash-wet steps leading down to a river of bodies, some only half digested by the funeral pyre, bodies of soggy dead dogs, their yellowish tongues drowning in the garbage-topped water. How could loneliness last longer than death, when death erased away everything, both longing and loneliness, once and for all? However wrong my idea, I knew I was right anyway; right beyond reason, which tells us so little, in any case. Somehow, I was certain that loneliness would find a way to penetrate our atoms as we whirl pointlessly about the endless universe endlessly. And, of course, where there was loneliness, there would also be longing.

"Why are you so wasteful of life, then," the waiter asked, "knowing what the ending brings and does not bring?"

Before I could answer, a young man detached himself from his table across the way and came up to our waiter in a huff.

"Don't you see us here?" he asked. "We've been waiting for ten minutes."

"Waiting for hours," a young woman shouted. "Tell him, waiting for hours." She wore a red scarf, which she twisted about her neck as if to strangle herself—either from impatience or to protest her waiting. One reason or another, she would do herself in, pronto, she signaled, unless the waiter showed up and took their order and brought them drinks. It takes some so little to want to die.

These were the same crowd, I imagined, who earlier had been cavorting outside in the snow, and who now were cavorting in the lounge, harmless and having fun, later to go somewhere—maybe in this very hotel—go and fuck, as the young do, without imagination. Of course, they do not need imagination.

"Oh! I'll come over soon," he said in the nicest way, not a waiter but an old friend table-hopping and promising he'd soon stop by for a visit.

Once, when I was dining with Henry, he whispered to

me as the young waiter left our table, "Isn't he beautiful? So beautiful."

"Stop it, Henry," I said. "Don't you think of anything else?"

"Don't you?"

He was right there, of course. When not thinking lofty thoughts or worried about bills and rent and how the lofty thoughts would pay for them, when not thinking what I was going to eat for dinner and where, what else did I think about, care about, dream about? In truth, the boy was beautiful, but I was annoyed to admit it. Annoyed with myself for admiring him, just arrived, I imagined, from a beach in Brazil, where I pictured him as he swam and tanned himself all day and made love to girls in a corrugated metal shed peppered by hot afternoon rain. Annoyed with myself for wanting to be him, desired by men and women, boys and girls, by the sun and its invisible, licking rays.

Then the waiter, our waiter, took a large white handkerchief from his pocket, displaying it like a bullfighter his cape, first to us and then to the impatient table.

OFF DUTY read the bold block letters.

I wondered whether he worked at his drollery.

"Do you have more handkerchiefs with other such messages?" I asked.

"I stay within bounds," he said.

"All right, let's have another round, please, and we'll call it a night," she said.

"Okay," he said. "Call it a night."

The girl who had feigned hanging herself came over. She had narrow shoulders and big breasts in a red sweater. She pulled her shoulders back when she addressed our waiter. She took my attention but he did not seem especially drawn. She smiled her young smile: Miles of life still ahead; miles of dicks still ahead, it said.

"Won't you come over now?" she asked, in what I took for a southern accent, the inflection of all sweetness. "We're all ready to order." The suicide-by-hanging ploy had not worked and now her charm was brought into service. It was considerable, her charm, and had I been the waiter, I would have taken her order then and there and I would have charged her tab to the house or paid it myself, but then again, I've always been a fool for the South.

"Off duty," he said, as if speaking to a silver nightingale on a jade bough fairway, in an old Chinese pagoda perched high over a misty waterfall. Perhaps that was where he went each time he left us, to revisit faraway, ancient places where he had once served.

"Well, then, good night," I said, "and many thanks for the drinks. And now we're on our way."

"Until later," he said.

He was droll, but how much drollery can one entertain in an evening, especially when what I imagined waiting for us in our room was so much more compelling than drollery?

I signed the chit and took her now-very-warm hand and led her to the elevator and finally up to our suite. The bed was made and the room freshened up since we had left that afternoon; a valley of roses scented the room; on the pillows, little bouquets of sweets wrapped in cellophane tied with a golden cord; on a faux Louis Quatorze table by the salmon-curtained window, a basket of fruit with a little note from the manager saying how pleased he was we had chosen to be the hotel's guests; how it would please him to please us further during our stay. I should have liked this place, cushioned from the pushy street, from ignorant noise, from disgusting odors, from reminders of how small, how inelegant we are in our daily life. But the little bags of sweets, the flowers, the faux Louis Quatorze table, the solicitous manager only saddened me—sensing in them attempts to sugarcoat our brief residency and eventual departure, sugarcoating, like beauty, death's disguise. Portentous.

I lay back in bed watching her undress. She enjoyed seeing me narrow my eyes and start to breath through my mouth, slowly, inhaling her. When I was young, I thought, as the young do, that when people grew older they no longer thought of sex, having somehow outgrown—matured beyond—the drive, serenity and a kind of neutered wisdom having slowly crept into its exciting place.

But here I was—by my earlier lights—an old man in a hotel, watching, as if for the very thrilling first time, a woman undress. Imagine, then, what more passionate and interesting a world it would be were we always starting anew, each day, with another lover, and each day or night burning with the mystery of a new body. She, for example, could have said to me that she liked the waiter and would I mind waiting over my drink while she took him up to our room and fucked him. What harm would it have done and what would it have meant except her pleasure, which there is so little of in life and an abundance of none after death?

"All right," I said aloud. "If not each day, then each week."

"What are you talking about?" she asked, her breasts heavy on my chest. Of course, Henry would have said "new young body." Well why not, while in the realm of dreams, why not dream?

"Oh! Nothing," I said. "Just blabbering until you came to bed."

"Did you mind my chatting up the waiter?" she asked. "I was just having fun, passing the time."

"First we pass time, then time passes us," I said.

"Why don't we just let time pass itself, and we'll stay where we are?" she said, giving my nipple a lick. "Unless you have another idea."

"Years ago," I said, my mind adventuring on its own, "I read a book called *Love's Body*. Do you remember that book? Or maybe I have it mixed up with Marcuse's book *Eros and Civilization*. It goes like this: One day, when we are free completely from all need to work, the body will regain its position—lost after early childhood—as a total organ of pleasure. Instead of having all our sensual and sexual gratification localized in the genital areas, so that we may remain undisturbed to work in society, one day the whole body will be liberated in polymorphic rapture."

"Sure," she said, moving off from me to her own pillow. "Another crackpot Utopian vision of life after socialism reaches its highest stage of development."

"Well, why stop there?" I said, bypassing her comment. "Shouldn't the destination of human progress include the totality of pleasure, of love? Shouldn't we finally free our-selves of the tyranny of gender differences? What a loss of love, loving just the opposite sex. Don't you think? How much time is there to live, after all? And why pass it away in such constraints?"

"Haven't you ever made love to a man?" she asked.

"No."

"Why not?"

"That physical part never really moved me, not in my guts. Though more than once I thought I should make love with Henry, because it would have pleased him."

"Well, you can't please everyone," she said.

"That's the sad point, almost."

"Maybe I should get dressed again and go look for our waiter," she said, in a not-unfriendly way, "and you can stay here and make love to your total organ."

"No," I said, putting my hand inside her thigh. "Not tonight, why waste the snow?"

She knew what I meant, even if I didn't. And soon we were alone with ourselves, swimming in an igloo scented with roses and brine. For a while I didn't love anyone in the world but her or anything in the world but this moment, knowing that all other moments before were spent marking time for this one.

We kissed several times in our half sleep and held each other, two babes in the hotel, while the world sped about us, churning in light and darkness. Then we finally fell asleep, thigh to thigh, under the warm stillness of our quilt.

I slept wonderfully until sometime in the night when the air conditioner went on by itself. The room was chilly and I meant to get out of bed and turn the damn thing off, but I was hoping it would do it all by itself because I was so cozy in bed, in my agreeable climate under the quilt. Just when it started to get uncomfortably cold and when I was about to jump ship into the icy waters, so to speak, the air conditioner did what I had earlier hoped and shut itself down. But even with it off, and even with my pressing myself to her, I did not seem to get warmer.

I cupped my hands over my dick, which felt the coldest part of me, after having been the warmest only some while ago. Once, in Peru, I saw a Mayan terra-cotta sculpture of a Death's head holding his erection. It was so funny, I thought, Death getting it up, but what, I wondered, would be there to excite, to stiffen him, when all of him was dead? And then as the snow was falling outside and in the silence of the chilled room, I conjectured that what got Death hot was Life, all of it, its being and its idea, which outlasts the last breath of the last atom. How many paintings, which I had carried—like a little portable museum—in my mind, and how many memories of women, whose aromas, whose voices, whose always young bodies I had memorized, would I take with me down to the grave or up with me in flames, and which would then imprint themselves forever in the marrow of the world?

It was five by the red dial of the clock on the night table; I checked because I could not comprehend why someone would be knocking at the door at that hour. Not a banging knock but a soft one, polite, as if not to disturb or wake the occupant of the room while of course intending to do exactly that. I put on the hotel's bathrobe and opened the door slightly, being sure to draw the little chain across it. It was hard at first to see what was there, because it was so obviously him that I did not at first register exactly what I was seeing.

"What is it?" I asked. Meaning, of course, Why are you here?

"Would you step out into the hallway, please?" he said. Very sweetly, as if I had vastly overtipped him and he was coming to makes things right.

"Why?" I asked foolishly, as if it were normal that he was there to begin with. Then I added, "Is something wrong?"

"Oh! No, nothing wrong at all. But do come out, I'd rather not like to wake your wife."

I was struck by the stilted diction—"rather not like to wake your wife."

What late-night, black-and-white movie classics of butlers in phony English country houses had he been watching? I wondered. But he made sense. I would not want to wake her, to rouse her, to frighten her.

We began walking down the empty corridor to the elevator bank; he took me by the arm gently, as if to help or lead me. Strangely, I was not disturbed by his familiarity but found it touching. Soon we were in the elevator and soon we were in the empty lobby and in a flash, it seemed, we were out the revolving door and into the snowy street, now empty and without a bus or cab in sight.

And soon we were strolling through Central Park, as if it were spring. I wasn't cold any longer and I began to imagine rows of daffodils and their waves of waxy sun where now there was snow covering the fields. I turned to tell him that. He was younger than when I first saw him in the hotel bar, younger by years and more beautiful. That was the word that came to me.

"I thought you were off duty," I said.

"But not for you," he said in the most solicitous way.

"All our lives, I thought we wait for you, but I now realize," I said, trying to make a joke, "you wait for us, you're the waiter."

"Oh! Yes," he said, "certainly." I could see he was distracted and his answer had no feeling.

"Look over there," he said, pointing to the Met, heavy in the dark snow, but spotted with little lights in glass windows. "That's one of the places you love, isn't it?" he added.

"It's one of them, along with the Louvre and the Prado," I said. "But it's the paintings, their beauty, I love, not where or what houses them."

"Yes," he said, "I know, and I would add that it's not even the paintings themselves you finally love, 'because love desires nothing bodily, but seeks beauty—but it happens that beauty can be nothing corporeal.'"

"What an elegant idea," I said, "and an ancient one, and serving nothing but one's wish never to die."

"Well, however that may be," he said, "let's sit here on this bench. Let's watch the snow falling and the trees swaying their icy dead branches and let's remain still while all about us speeds and churns."

And so we did.

The Bar on
Tompkins Square Park
Self Portrait with Blue Horse

"Let's not stay much longer," she said.

"Bored already? We just got here."

"It's tired here. It was tired from the minute we walked in."

"You chose the place, didn't you?"

"Sure, but that doesn't make it any less tired, does it?"

She had straight brunette hair with a few flecks of gray. She had the jade-green eyes of an Aztec jaguar. She had white skin and full lips, red without lipstick. She had a creamy neck. She had narrow shoulders. I liked these and other of her features but that was not why I loved her.

"Okay, let's leave, then," I said.

"Well, let me finish my drink, at least!"

I thought it best to say nothing for a while. She sipped her highball stuffed with fresh mint and ice. A summer drink, incongruous with the present season. She wore a thin yellow wool sweater with short sleeves. I could feel the cold on her naked arms.

A blind man in his early thirties put change in an old juke-box, then returned to his seat at the bar. He did not use his cane or his dog to find his way to and fro in the bar, so you would hardy know he was sightless were it not for the round coal-black glasses framing his very pale face or for the dog with its harness beside him on the stool.

"How are you, Harry?" I asked.

His dog pricked up his ears and glanced my way, blinking. He often answered to his master's name, though his moniker was Augustus.

"Not bad, Louie. Just sailing with the days," the blind man said, looking my way.

"Fair winds, then, Harry," I said, turning to her, who was gently pressing her glass against her cheek.

"Toothache again?" I asked her.

"Toothache for love, toothache for that root canal you promised me for my last birthday."

"It's considered unethical for a dentist to drill his lover—unless he bills her," I said.

"Bill away, Bill. And please order my drink in the meanwhile."

I motioned to the barman, who I could see was not wanting to be bothered with work, filling in, as he was, little boxes with words in a newspaper he had spread across the bar.

Finally, I made a polite wave.

"What's your desire, Marie?" he addressed her with a full smile of yellow teeth.

"The usual," she said, "is my desire."

And presently he filled a quarter of a water glass with amber stuff, poured out from a bottle with her name inked on the label.

"What about you, Louie?" he asked, with the weariness of a man who had woken that morning to find his life had taken a walk without him.

"Another java, maybe in a glass this time."

"Someone was asking about your paintings last week," he said, giving a nod to a seascape of mine on the wall. Sailboats caught in a squall, masts heeling seaward, the sky pewter, the sun frightened.

"Asking what?"

"The same as always."

"Did you remember to mention that I might be flexible about the price?"

"No. I said they were not for sale and that he could not afford them if they were."

"Perfect."

The blind man walked to the piano in the rear and began tickling the ivories, which soon got giddy with melody. Augustus remained by the stool, coolly guarding his master's seat.

A blue horse walked into the bar and asked for a beer, but

since he was a known deadbeat and a flagrant nontipper, the bartender pretended not to notice him and slid over to the opposite end of the bar, where, stashed in a white vase, a bouquet of sixteen white roses drooped, having seen better days weeks ago.

Snow began to press lightly against the window—a snow of bloody feathers torn from pigeons murdered in flight by the local hawks. But soon more snow fell, this time the glacial kind, forged by all manner of precipitation and atmospheric changes. Flat gray sky, white snowflakes in a whirl describing the letter *M*. I ordered my third coffee, in a cup this time.

A couple walked into the bar. She wore a tight red dress and red pumps. Her hair was red, so, too, her Italian leather handbag melting in softness. He was just a flat guy, you could hardly see him when he turned sideways. Otherwise, it is useless to describe him because you would forget what he looks like the instant you finished the sentence describing him. At least I would. He had the voice of a rasp being tickled by straw. And in that voice he ordered a ginger ale with a water backer. She ordered the same but in reverse.

"Why couldn't you just say you'd have the same?" He glanced at me to let me know he was irritated with her. As if to say, Women from the time of Mother Eve to Madame Curie are irritating. They stir up trouble in gardens and bull rings, radiate grief and disorder in restaurants and bars. I did not return him a concurring look because to some degree

I like trouble and grief and disorder organized by women. Intelligent women. Witty women. Sexy women. Women who wear hats with half veils at cocktail parties. Women who walk as if stalking a rose. Women who, when you are about to take a long walk off a short pier, might say, "May I tag along?" Women: Marie.

"The order in which drinks appear is important to me," the woman in red said. "I like the water set down before the G A."

"The G A?"

"You say B and B, so what's the diff?"

He saw her point and backed down. I would have done the same, back down at her argument. I have always wanted to be reasonable.

The clock struck three. Then moved on to chew up another hour. To chew off another bit of my life. Chew up all the life about us, the hawks of Avenue B, the elm trees in the park, the worn oak wood of the bar, the horse with his two missing front teeth, the woman in the red dress with half her finger poked in a glass of water, the man with the raspy voice nervously searching for some item in his jacket's left breast pocket. His anxiety infected me and made me search my pocket to be reassured that my little box of pills was still there—which it was.

The horse swung his mane impatiently. A few of us at the bar wished he would leave because he was always taking up too much air and space, even on a wide Monday afternoon. And always being glum and sending out currents of gloominess.

But, for the moment, I felt sorry for the sorry nag and I said, "Send him a beer—float over a bucket, in fact; I'm buying."

I was high on cash, but I could have put the bill on my tab. My tab was good anywhere, even in the Bronx, where the sky is poor, except on Sunday family dinners ages ago when I was a boy and my Uncle Umberto magically plucked dimes from my ear. What made me think of that now? The Bronx and the dead. My dead piled up there in Woodlawn Cemetery waiting for me. The barman made a few polite swipes of his towel and settled a bucket before the horse. Eddie, for that was the jade's name, made a little bow my way before dunking his head in the bucket of suds.

Then Marie said sweetly, "Do you think we could go to the movies this evening?"

"And your husband?"

"I'm sure he'd join us if you ask."

"He didn't the last time."

"That doesn't mean he won't want to go this time."

"Right you are, why didn't I think of that?"

We were just going through an old routine. She had no husband and she hated the movies. I like them all, from *A Day at the Races* to *The Third Man*, especially the movies in which all the actors in them are dead. Ghosts on the screen, saying the same lines and doing the same deeds for eternity. A kind of afterlife in which we the living share with them.

It comes at you quickly. One morning you wake up and find a hard lump in your throat, or you get a stunning headache that no aspirin can alleviate, or in a routine physical exam they find spots on your pancreas or insoluble fiber meshed in your lungs or cancer swimming in your blood, singing in your liver. One morning you wake to a death sentence without any hope of reprieve or pardon; and from that morning on you are already dead in an ocean of the living. These may be platitudes, but are true nonetheless.

The flat man came over, a little shy a little cautious a little smiling a little stooped over in deference. Looking only at me, he said:

"Pardon me for bothering you."

Don't bother me, then you wouldn't have to be pardoned, I wanted to say, for the joke of it, but of course I didn't say that: "No bother," I said affably. What does it cost, affability?

"My girlfriend wanted me to ask if your lady friend is an actress she thinks she recognizes from the movies."

"Very likely," I said. "Marie is a great star of the Bulgarian cinema."

"Bulgaria. Where the Bulgars live," Marie joined in, affecting a French accent.

"She'll be happy to know she was right," the flat man said, backing away to deliver the news.

I motioned to the barman, who some while ago had traded the crossword puzzle for a scratch sheet.

"Send them over a round or two of whatever they're having, please."

"On your tab?" He wasn't pressing me, just wanted to get

the billing straight. He was one of the few left who did not care that much about money but cared about the form of things.

"No," I said, "it's cash today, and I'll settle my account before we leave."

I liked the manly fullness of saying the words, "I'll settle my account." I would have liked to have had the occasion to have said it more often and with such variation as "let's settle our accounts" or "let's call it quits."

"Who you betting on, Lorenzo?" I asked the barman with polite curiosity.

"On some losing nag or another," he said with a little sigh.

The blue horse flicked his ears, flared his nostrils, made huffing noises. "We are not nags," he said with equine dignity. "And we do not enjoy talk about or reference to glue factories in our presence, should you ever have the mind to bring up those dreadful places in immediate conversation."

"I apologize sincerely," Lorenzo said. "Please accept another bucket or two with my best wishes."

The horse gave a nod and a little lift of his foreleg. "Okay. All's jake with us, all's level, L.," he said.

Augustus came by and gave me and Marie quite a sniffing. He always had favored Marie and took an extra whiff of her shoes, finding some world of interest there. Maybe it was some traces of Kublai Kahn's pulverized bones that had drifted over the Steppes, over oceans and deserts and amber time that he had smelled, or maybe it was the dried urine of a man who, caught short of home one winter night, of necessity peed against a tree, an elm of great age and bearing, like the one in Tompkins Square Park diagonally facing my apartment window.

"Lorenzo," I said, "can you find Augustus a chunk of baloney in the fridge?"

"He doesn't appreciate baloney," Harry called out, giving the keys a rest. "But I do."

"Fix Harry a sandwich, would you please, L.?" I said, tiring of calling him by his full name and following Eddie's earlier abbreviation. "On me, of course."

The woman in red came over to thank me for her drink. But she had her eyes on Marie.

"I've never seen a Bulgarian film, so that's probably not where I've seen her."

Time chewing up Augustus, too. Ticking away at his bones, at his dreams. Why is it, I wondered, that there are speaking horses but no speaking dogs? And what kind of dreams did he have, that Augustus, a seeing-eye dog, responsible, always on duty, careful, cautious, bound to his blind man for life? Did Augustus ever dream of adventures in which he ran wild, without leash, in streets and in parks with others of his kind?

"You should try," I said, "seeing one the next time there's a Bulgarian film festival. Bulgarian cinema is great and noble and generally underlit, but to stunning effect."

She smiled, graciously, I thought, or graciously enough to make me feel foolish for having persisted in this lame joke.

"What would you like to hear?" Harry asked, throwing his voice in my direction.

"Choose something you like, Marie," I said. "Whatever it is, I know I'll like it, too."

"I wish I had a guy like that," the woman in red said, nodding my way, to the flat man in a voice loud and wistful.

"See?" Marie said. "I always told you there's a woman waiting for you somewhere."

"Rather unwieldy title for a song, don't you think?"

The snow was falling heavily in the park. Perhaps elsewhere as well. The snow was falling in thuds that I could not hear. The snow was covering the benches. The snow was . . . was white! Also a little purple because of the purple of the dying light. Also a little violet. Purple and violet, yes.

Marie went over to the piano and whispered in Harry's ear. Harry smiled and spread his fingers percussively over the keys and soon the bar was filled with piano music of romantic distinction. First "Smoke Gets in Your Eyes," followed by, as Marie had also obviously requested, "Just Plain Bill," then concluding with "Louie Louie."

Not a dry eye in the house. Even Eddie shed a long tear or two down his great long face. Marie went to the loo to wipe the mascara off her cheeks but before she left she said with the warmest of smiles, "Don't let that lady in red give you any ideas, Louie. You belong to me."

"Day and night," I said. "Night and day."

What a good end to the day, what more perfect way to leave it behind? To know that Marie also had a good time with me at the bar meant the world. Before long, I would send her home in a taxi and know she would soon arrive in her cozy flat someplace over the Brooklyn Bridge and be there safe from the mounting snow and the bitter cold that bites the empty streets near rivers. I would take a walk through Tompkins Square Park, passing by the children's slides and swings, and find my way to a bench facing the row of brownstones on Tenth Street, and look up to my lighted apartment window.

Eddie came over to me and in a very low voice said, "Louie, may I have a word with you alone?"

"Shoot," I said.

It was a story about a horse he knew, who had told him a story about a horse *he* knew, a story about a race that was soon to happen.

"Okay," I said, without too much enthusiasm. I had already heard the one about the horse who needed a cataract operation and was too broke to pay for it. I wished Marie would soon return to rescue me. She didn't give Eddie the time of day in these philanthropic matters and would gently brush off any of his appeals and schemes.

"This horse I know knows a horse who is going to win at Aqueduct. It is certain."

"Wonderful," I said. "I hope you make a bundle on the bet."

"Not just me, but you, too!"

Then he let me have it: He needed a loan. The bet was sure sure sure, and he'd repay me immediately plus interest. He insisted on the interest.

"The odds?"

"That's the beauty part. Thirty-to-one."

"Does this winner have a name?"

"Lightning."

"The greased or the plain variety?"

"Look, Louie, it's a fabulous deal," Eddie said.

"No question. I even like the odds." I took the wad from my pocket and peeled off ten one-hundreds under the counter. "This is for you, Eddie." Then I counted off another grand and said, "This is for me. But if I forget to collect the winnings, give them to Marie."

Eddie gave me a long, thoughtful sway of his head. Touching in its duration. Then in a low, earnest tone he said, "I'll be back here tomorrow at five with everything, Louie."

"I'm sure you will," I said, and I was.

Marie came back just as Eddie was returning to his place. He gave her a gallant nod. And she returned his salute with an affectionate pat on his shoulder.

"He's okay," she said when he left. "What did he want this time?"

"He came to tell me how beautiful you looked today but he was too shy to tell you himself."

She smiled. "He's not bad-looking, but he could use some grooming."

"I'm sure he'd glam himself up under the right circumstances."

"Like you did," she said, smiling, brushing her fingers over my face.

It was dark now. The snow was blowing about crazily under the streetlights. I knew it was freezing outside. I could feel it even in the quiet, mellow warmth of the bar. I thought it was getting to be time. I thought that even if I could sit there with Marie forever I could not. How could I keep on delaying and delaying?

"Let's just have something here," I said. "I can't face going out and looking for a place to eat. It's so cold out there tonight."

"Good idea," Marie said. "Just something little, I don't care."

"Yes, let's do that, then I put you in a cab."

"Are you coming?"

"I'd love to," I said, "but I can't tonight."

"I'm disappointed," she said, making a disappointed face. Seeing her expression almost made me change my mind—not that it would have mattered.

We ate some heated-over tomato soup and kaiser rolls. A crummy dinner that put us in a down mood. Everyone at the bar was in a down mood, reluctant to leave, tired of staying. But slowly they drifted out, the blind man and his dog, the flat man with the woman in red. Eddie with a thick wool shawl over him that Lorenzo had found in the back room.

And we left, too. I kissed Marie as I normally would, not

too hard and not too passionately, as I very much would have wanted. I watched the cab stop at a light, the snow piling up on the back window, where I thought I glimpsed Marie waving at me. Then the cab took off, grinding away down the snowy street until it disappeared into a whirling cloud of whiteness.

The Park on Fire

The plane was still circling low over the city, its silvery wings flashing into my eyes, the whirl of its propeller roaring over the hum of my thoughts. I walked along the avenue, passing families with happy children, lovers on their Sunday stroll. A few pointed to the flying relic or to the other one hurtling toward us like a spear with teeth. Except for their low altitude, the streets were indifferent; but for their drone, the sky was untroubled, the air crystal, the sun in full fire.

My walk took me into a forested park above the city, and I soon left behind the planes. Left behind, too, my little hotel and my wife in it, reading in bed, happy in her own company for the while. I could see her, still in pajamas, a pot of warm coffee on the night table, a book on the cultivation of roses in hand. "One day, we will have a garden," she said. "And I will grow only roses, and live only for you and my roses."

Pink roses along a white fence, roses bordering the window of my study, where I would read in a deep leather chair, my bookshelves high to the ceiling, my carpet thick and deadening the world's noise. One day, one day.

I walked higher and higher and deeper into the park for what seemed forever, until I came upon a band of children playing hide-and-seek, their parents eyeing them from park benches and tall wicker chairs like open black coffins. A blindfolded boy counted numbers in the hundreds while his companions hid impatiently behind bushes and trees, waiting, waiting for him to tear off his blindfold and to begin pursuing them.

So absorbed was I by the children and their playful screams that I hardly noticed the young couple sitting on the bench opposite me. But then I saw their eye beams intertwine like enamored vines in the sun.

"Do you love me?" she asked.

"Oh! No," he said. "Do you love me?"

"Not at all."

"I suppose we do not love each other, then?" he said.

"Only sometimes, on Sunday afternoons in August," she answered, looking at her watch as if to check the hour.

"I'm in despair," he said, "thinking of all the other loveless days in my life." She laughed, like a flash of sun on a hospital window. They kissed and, hand in hand, disappeared into a cove of bushes, a breeze of youth and crushed jasmine in their wake.

Seeing them made me happy, in a restless way. Happy for their youth and for all their time ahead to be foolish and oblivious to the endings of anything, let alone to the end of love. I was happy for myself, too, for the pleasure of being in a green park on a bench glazed with light. For the moment, I would not allow the planes overhead, seemingly from nowhere, to break my serenity.

Looking about me I thought: Everywhere, now and on every Sunday to come, in every park in the Western world, parents are watching their children at play. Everywhere in park coves and sheltering woods lovers are embracing, mindless of the traffic of planes and people. Everywhere planes are roaring over museums, muting the talk of paintings in the galleries below. Everywhere in hotels, in apartments grand and sad, in homes dark and bright, wives are waiting for their husbands while propellers bite into the sky.

I left the screaming children and the blindfolded boy still at his endless count and wandered through the park until I found myself at a fountain where Neptune sat on concrete waves, his trident poised above a concrete sea and three nymphs swimming under his thrall. I paused and, with my eyes closed, listened to the fountain's gentle splash, feeling the day's embracing warmth.

I considered lingering there, letting flow the memories of when I went down to the sea as a young man filled with dreams. I was unafraid of the world then, or of unfamiliar streets, or unknown ports, unafraid of history, which I had believed would one day lead me and the whole turbulent world to the Great Harmony, the dialectical end of human strife, which only strife could engender. But the idea of my remaining—like an idolater—by the fountain did not last very long before the incessant roar of planes broke my reverie and sent me deeper into the mazelike park.

It was so lovely walking in the silent, green shade of trees that I granted my thoughts free range, leaving the day to take me wherever it would. I was deep into my quiet when I heard jeering and harsh voices from within a clump of glistening holly bushes. Then the sounds of someone crying in pain, followed by men laughing derisively.

"Suck on this, suck it," one shouted.

I peered into the brush and saw three men in 1930s military uniforms kicking, each in turn, a youngish man doubled up on the ground.

"Take a lick of this, poet," the tallest of the three said, unbuttoning his trousers.

"Paint it green," one said. "He loves everything green."

"Enough of this boring shit," the third and shortest one said. "Take him to the car and finish him down the road."

They gave him another round of kicks and lifted him away

through the brush, leaving a trail of pages in their wake. Poems, they were, ripped from a notebook. I pocketed as many as I could, then rushed away to find help. One of the three soldiers emerged from the bushes, barring my way.

"Your papers," he said.

I showed him my passport, which he examined as if it were an alien document. Then in a flash he gave me a terrific slap.

"What is this joke?" he said, opening the flap of his pistol holster.

I started to protest when his officer called out from the brush. "Leave him alone or shoot him."

"I think he saw certain things," the soldier answered.

"Who cares? Look at him! Don't you see he's crazy?"

The soldier looked me up and down—perhaps to assess just how crazy I was—and began to laugh. "Where did you get those ridiculous clothes?" he asked.

The slap was bad enough, I almost said, but now you've pushed this too far! I had, after all, always been considered well dressed, elegant even. *Un homme classic*, my future bride once said of me to a mutual friend. What made me think of that compliment just then, when a soldier had just slapped me and had reached for his pistol, a soldier who had been kicking a man until blood ran from his ears and nose?

My clothes! Look at you with your phony movie uniform, I started to say, before he turned, still laughing, and ran to join his companions.

I continued walking rapidly, hoping to find the police and report the assault, but I seemed to be walking to nowhere. Nevertheless, I reasoned that if I stayed along the same path, it would eventually lead me to where I could find help.

Sure enough, I soon entered a lush field of tombstones. It was curious, I thought, that a park path would lead into a cemetery—but there it was. Not a very grand or ancient cemetery—like Père Lachaise, where you feel small, as if your well-intentioned life and modest achievements had amounted to nothing when compared to all those distinguished dead buried in its confines. This cemetery was a reassuring place, with soft hills and tall cypress trees. A cemetery like the neighborhood park where I spent my childhood days playing under the protective eye of a grandmother I loved.

There was comfort here, but also, I reasoned, where there are cemeteries there must be roads leading from and to populated streets—or how else would the living and the dead ever find their way to each other? I was reassured, too, by the sounds of the backfiring of cars and trucks, evidence of how close I was to the city and how I would soon find myself back to its heart.

The two were sitting on a stone bench under the shade of a weeping willow, though there was no need for shade, the sun having already started to cool, taking the diamond light along with it.

The old man looked up first. "I always wondered," he said, "if I would live long enough to see it."

"I was always sure you would," she said, caressing his hand.

"And now it is wonderfully arriving," he said, with a sweet tremble in his voice. His hair was white and amazingly thick for a man clearly in his nineties. His double-breasted suit—with a little spiked-hammer pin on the lapel—looked newly tailored for an embassy dance in Berlin or in some smart Art Deco club in Paris between the two world wars.

I was relieved to see them, thinking that I would ask for a lift in the car that had taken them to the cemetery.

"You have brought me luck, young man," he said.

"And luck for me, too," I said, turning with a smile to the beautiful young woman beside him.

Amazing how beauty quickens the heart and makes it foolish. I was ashamed of myself for flirting with her, feeling I had betrayed my wife, who by now must be worrying about me, my walk lasting longer than anyone could have dreamed. Everywhere, I thought, wives are waiting while their husbands are dawdling in cemeteries among newly dug graves.

Before I could say another foolish word, there was a soft thump at my feet. A dead bird had fallen from the tree, then another, then others—little sparrows with burned beaks littering the green.

"That it would come one day, I also believed," she said, disregarding me and my intended compliment, "but perhaps not arrive so soon." She kissed the old man's hand.

"What day is that?" I asked.

"When the world is finally brought to order," she said.

"The last day of history," he added, not too gently.

What an absurd idea, I thought, because history ends only when all human life ends. What is the world but an ever-growing volume of histories? We are famished for stories old and new and would invent them even in our graves, even in our ashes. I was about to say all that when, in a flash, we were surrounded—minus parents and guardians— by the very children I had seen earlier playing hide-and-seek, the boy now wearing his blindfold tied about his neck militia-style.

"Children," she said, rising from the bench and reaching out her arms toward them, "the moment has come."

"How happy we are, happy happy happy," they shouted in chorus.

A plane flew overhead, then others followed, like a trail of steel geese, the grate of their engines sounding an overture to a mechanical symphony by that twentieth century composer who thought to end the old, bourgeois world of instrumental music and replace it with the clangs and violent harmonies of machines, with the beauty of the new world of engines and factory whistles.

"No more books," she said. "No more parents. Only the Guides," she added. The children applauded, their cries like singing knives. No one spoke or looked at me, but I felt the menace under their childish voices.

"I must be on my way," I said, more to myself than to anyone there. But no one seemed to care if I stayed or left, no one seemed to notice me, and no one said goodbye.

Children, I reflected, walking under the arching elms, have no history and are thus ideal for revolutionary armies. Everything old is their natural enemy. Old parents, old libraries, old teachers, old schools where they are trained to lie, and from whose stuffy rooms they one day emerge ancient, vibrant with fossilized ideas.

Didn't I myself once love the dream of washing away the old, the cleansing of its privilege, the destruction of every building of partisan law, every edifice of superstition, every stone of the old order, whose order meant misery for most and luxury for the few? But as I grew older, I came to admire everything old. Except for slavery, now perfected so that today's slaves imagine that by their industry they will be given a spacious room in their master's dreams.

I left the cemetery dispirited, the children's cries behind me. There was still much left of the day, I told myself, time enough to return to my hotel and to start my own history again, one with a blank sky and with my wife in my arms. It was with these thoughts that I found him there, still bleeding, crumpled against a tombstone at the cemetery's edge. He flinched when he saw me.

"I'm not with them," I said. "In fact, I want to help you."

He coughed up a small laugh. "Find my notebook, then," he said.

"First a hospital, I think."

"'This hospital, my life'—from an English poem, I think."

"I found these," I said, stuffing his pocket with the pages I had taken from the ground. He smiled and patted his pocket like a miser wanting to hear the reassuring clinks of gold coins.

"You need a doctor," I said.

"What time is it, anyway?" he asked, looking up at the sky.

"Approaching five," I said, citing a time I felt right for the mood of the day. *A las cinco de la tarde*, I wanted to add for the reference.

"I suspected as much. It's a brutal hour to be unlucky."

He lifted himself from the ground but fell back again, his head pillowed by the headstone. I thought it best he stay still, I said—as if I knew about these things—because he might be bleeding internally.

"Help me get to the museum," he continued. "I have to help save the paintings from burning."

"It's you who's burning—with fever," I said.

"The museum is under siege, it needs help; it needs every citizen to help evacuate the paintings," he said in a spiral of words.

"That was a lot of 'helps' in one sentence," I noted.

"A bouquet of helps," he said with a most charming smile. "They kicked the language out of me," he added.

"More than language," I suggested, "because I'm sure the museum is doing fine."

Another one of those quirks of speech, I thought: how does

a museum "do" anything? And what a strange time to wonder about oddities of language—when confronted by a bleeding man, and when I myself needed help to find my way home. Where was I now in this world? Where, indeed, was the world itself, and who was caring after it, as plane after plane sped overhead heating the sky with raw noise?

He looked weaker by the moment and I was afraid for him. "I'll go and find help," I said.

"Now you've caught the 'helps.'"

"I can't help myself," I answered. We laughed like old friends, which, in a sense, we were.

"I've long lived in the warmth of your poetry," I said, recognizing at last his handsome face. A grown man with a boy's sweet, hope-filled look; I was sure he would be pained at a sparrow's broken wing.

"You flatter me," he said, shielding his eyes. "But leaving me aside, is it not exciting how words can transport you, like flying carpets woven of syllables?"

"Even when I was a young man I read you, wondering how words could carry so much color as to change the complexion of sad buildings and brighten the black walls of poorhouses and prisons and lift the spirits of those committed there."

"Too kind of you," he said. "Though I fear you give undue weight to words, which surely tint the world but do not make it spin."

"I recited your lines when there was nothing and no one waiting for me. When no port was home."

"That's the best time for poetry," he said, "when you feel there is no one in the world waiting for you or thinking of you."

"When your only companions are the words on the page," I added.

"I suspect that would be true for you, especially now that you're alone again," he said.

"Not at all," I protested. "A woman I love is waiting for me."

But strangely, all that suddenly seemed long ago, that wife in a hotel, whom I left one morning to take a stroll in the park. She might still be waiting, but I wondered, at this pace of mine, if I would ever see her again. And if I did, would she still remember ever loving me? My thoughts were broken by the flight of crows overhead, so many crows screeching at such a black pitch that I had to cover my ears, until they passed on, leaving the sky picked clean like a child's skeleton.

At that moment, the young couple I had seen in the park earlier came toward me, arm in arm, smiling and disheveled. She had a little arrow-shaped twig stuck in her hair, which her lover removed gently and presented to her.

"A little souvenir," he said with a bow. She smiled, replacing it in her hair.

The poet laughed. "Look at you two doves! What a joy to know you have the good sense to go off to make love in the bushes when the city is under a furious cloud."

"I suspect half of the city is in the bushes," the young man said. "The other half were waiting for us to leave to take our places."

"Where else but the bushes? The hotels are packed to the windows," she said. "But soon even the hotels won't be safe, nowhere will be safe for love."

I looked down the alley of arching elms and thought: Everywhere lovers are driven out; everywhere lovers are searching for a bed above the clouds; everywhere lovers are looking up at a sky wallpapered with drunken planes and squadrons of shrieking crows.

"I was in the bushes myself," the poet said, laughing, "just a little while ago, with men who didn't know if they wanted to make love to me or kill me."

"Both, I think," I said.

"Poets are useful," he said, laughing again, "for forecasting the weather. When they come to kill us, it means that soon the skies will crash down on everyone."

"That may be true," the young man said anxiously, "but we can't stay here all day. We're going to help evacuate the paintings. But we got sidetracked."

She smiled. "Oh! Yes, and what a sweet detour that was."

I saw you both on the bench earlier, I wanted to say, flirting with each other although you knew duty called, and now you are in a big rush to leave the poet to die here with a stranger. But then, recalling the warmth with which the poet had just greeted them, I thought: Love commands before all other calls, the call we follow at all hours, at every age and in all domains, the call we long to hear, even on our deathbeds, at our last breath. The ocean may be violent, with lightning stabbing the rising waters, yet, at Neptune's bid, the nymphs swim up from the sea's cozy bed to wrap themselves about his giant thigh.

"One of us should stay with the poet," the young man said.

"You two go ahead," I said, thinking I would stay until help came our way or until the poet died.

Few have had the chance to sit with a great poet at his death, to hear his final words, and whether they are a yes or no for life. Keats's friend Severn stayed at the poet's bedside to record his final, exultant line. "I know it's my life," Keats exclaimed, coughing up blood into his white sheets, "but look at the color!"

My mind is stuffed with such anecdotes. Perhaps because I see history made of pieces, fragments—"intellectual bric-a-brac," my wife calls it. Easier for me to cipher out the world that way, I tell her. Thus, depending on my mood, on the color of the day, I can pull out an anecdote to prove this or that idea from the whole of our human history. Depending on my mood, see history as a record of progress or a journal of demises, a book of good or an anthology of horror. I wondered then, thinking back on Keats and of the poet before my eyes, who would be there to record the world's dying words and who would be left wishing to read them.

"We'll send a doctor to look after him," the young woman said.

"If there are any to be found at such a crazy time," her companion added. They made a quick retreat, vanishing down the path, her skirt swaying over her golden legs.

We remained together, the poet and I, the silence broken by the uneasy wind breathing through the cloudy cypress trees and the planes screaming overhead.

"It would be convenient to die here," the poet muttered, "because the transition to the grave is so direct. Just scoop a hole in the earth and roll me in."

"You're feverish," I said. "I'm going for help this minute."

"What could be more succinct," he continued, "less clotted with the boring exposition of funerals and ceremony? A death like an honest poem, lean and without decoration."

His eyes were fluttering and I thought to keep him awake for fear he would fall into a coma. But then I thought that should his assailants return, my staying by his side would come to no good for either of us. Let him sleep, I reasoned, until I return with a doctor. Let him dream. Let poets dream unhindered, until their dreams, like a vast screen of images, engulf and transform the world. I watched him a few minutes until I was sure he was breathing and deep into his sleep, and then I left for help.

"I'll pray for you," I said, thinking: Everywhere poets are sleeping, everywhere poets are fishing the ocean of dreams; everywhere poets are searching for the passwords to the brighter room; everywhere poets are trolling for infant images waiting to have faces; everywhere frightened hopes are tapping at the poet's window asking to be let in; everywhere murdered poems sail away like paper dolls in a breeze; everywhere lies slip under our doors like the shadows of letters; everywhere poets are singing above the shriek of planes.

I walked some while along a gravel path stained red and came upon a dark lake bounded by charred pines that climbed the sooty and burnt hills. In the distance, a crenellated tower sprouted long arms of orange fire, and on the opposite shore, two ancient cannons sent up powdery puffs of friendly-looking smoke. A skiff, carrying the two lovers, approached from the misty lake.

"I like lakes and I like rowing, but this is idiotic," he said as he disembarked.

"How is the poet?" she asked, looking about as if he might be there with me.

"Declining," I said. "And you, didn't you go for help?"

"Yes, of course we went," she said, "but every time we get to a point of crossing the lake those cannons fire on us. They have already blown up half the castle."

"It's a beautiful castle," I said. "Lancelot might have sequestered his beloved there when he stole her from his king."

"A castle only good for storing memories and old keys," he said.

"A castle for us when we were very young," she said, giving him a sharp look, "because then as now we had no place to go."

He shrugged his shoulders in a charming way, as if to say, I suppose we shall have to make the best of it.

"If they win, every couple will have to get married. You won't be allowed to see a naked breast until you get married," she said.

"Let's get married now, then," he said cheerfully. "Why run the risk of what happens later?"

"No marriage today or tomorrow or the day after."

"And why not, my beauty?"

"Because I do not love you," she said, with a heavenly smile that I wished she had sent me. I so much needed a loving smile to help me believe that I had not gone aground and that one day I would return to my wife and my peaceful home, where parks and old castles were not exploding in flames, where planes did not suffocate the sky and every free thought breathing in it.

"Let's go," he said, taking her hand. "If we can't cross the lake, we'll walk around it."

"The park is dangerous, packed with roving bands murdering everything that is not them," she said.

"Then let's go over the hills. What difference how long it takes us? Even if it takes a year or ten, as long as we're together."

"One day more than ten and I leave you," she said.

"I beg you to be careful," I said, feeling how much I had already come to like them.

"We'll make ourselves invisible," she said. "We can do everything together, even fly and walk on water." She took the little arrow twig from her hair. "Here," she said to me, "a little memento of your travels and a talisman to keep you safe."

Her lover kissed her on the cheek. "She's my protector. And she'll protect you, too," he said to me. "Just come along with us."

I was tempted to join them but there is nothing to make you feel more lonely than being with lovers wrapped in their dream. "Thank you," I said. "I'll take my chances on the lake."

She kissed me on both cheeks. "We shall see you again." The young man shook my hand, then, as an afterthought, hugged me in the warm way of old comrades.

I watched them march into the forest of burnt pines and prayed for their safety until they were dots in the charred distance. Then I took to the skiff. I rowed for long minutes, rowing, rowing, the oarlocks squeaking like mice broken in traps; all else had gone silent now, the cannons were napping, the breeze had fallen asleep in the trees. I rowed until finally I came upon the burning castle, where, on the adjacent terrace, three men—their faces red with smoke and ash—sat silently working at a round wooden table.

The old man was among them but was much younger than when I had last seen him in the cemetery, now seemingly in his strong forties. He had given up his pin-striped suit and was in a flowing black robe—like a wizard in King Arthur's days. The little silver hammer which had adorned his lapel earlier was now life-sized and blood-flecked in his hand.

"It's less constraining than a suit," he said, when I noted

the change in his attire, "and more befitting our time." His companions, similarly dressed, did not even look up, busy as they were ripping leaves from books, shredding them and mixing the scraps into three bowls of brown porridge.

"Have some," he said, offering me a bowl. "You must be hungry after so long a day."

"Not hungry," I said.

"In any case, it's better to fatten the pig first," the one with a shaved head said, still not looking up. The other, a red-nosed man, laughed and stirred his bowl with a long wooden spoon.

"Where is your granddaughter?" I asked, supposing she was that.

"Who?" he asked.

"The young lady you were with earlier," I said, retreating from my question.

"Thinking about her?" he asked slyly. "Even in times like these?"

I was embarrassed, feeling I had again betrayed my wife, because my inquiry was not made from politeness but from a wish to see that beautiful woman once again.

"What do you think," the red-nosed man asked me suddenly, "which tastes the more bitter, the Mill or the Marx?"

"It's a perfectly fair test," the other said, pushing the bowls before me, "because you don't know which bowl contains which."

"In any case," the once-old man said, "we have finally found the way to turn the world's boring shit into the good."

"Soon," the shaved head said, "we'll have shredders to pulp all the books in the world."

"And with the compost, we'll fertilize a million trees, each taller than eternity," added the red-nosed man. "Their branches leaved with hanged bodies."

"Here," the rejuvenated old man said, thrusting into my hand a page he had just torn from an open volume. "Read," he added sternly, in a voice like my Latin teacher's when he pressed me for my translation of Cicero's *De re publica*. Me, standing, unprepared, frightened, book in hand, at the rear of the classroom, by a window giving to a black courtyard heaped with greasy winter coal. That was an innocent long ago, when a teacher's disapproval had the power to cloud my day and blight my sleep. But the voice of authority must still have had some sway over me because I obediently began to read aloud:

" 'The materialist conception of history starts from the principle that production, and with production, the exchange of its products, is the basis of every social order; that in every society which has appeared in history the distribution of the products, and with it the division of society into classes or estates, is determined by what is produced and how it is produced, and how the product is exchanged.' "

It was a text I had long forgotten, one that in my youth I had believed held the key to all human conduct and to everything that would guide it to harmony.

The cannons began booming again, thundering out my

voice, and so I stopped reading, though I wondered all along why I had allowed myself to be bullied into reading in the first place.

"Did we order you to stop?" the red-nosed man asked.

"He's read enough anyway," the shaved-head man said. "Now let him eat it with his porridge."

"Like a good boy," the young-old man said.

"I don't think so," I said. "I must be on my way." I suffered at my weak reply.

They laughed. "Run along before the bad wolves get you," the red-nosed man said.

"Where will he run?" the young-old man said. "It's a forest of wolves out there."

"Wolves with scissors for teeth," the shaved head added.

This made them laugh even more. I quickly got into my skiff and rowed away without a goodbye—a small defiance.

I rowed until the three were smudges on a terrace of smoke and orange flames, rowed until I came to a lush bank, cool in a green breeze, and silent, as if the airplanes had disappeared and the cannons, too. All that noise and those flames were now behind me and I was sure that soon I would find my way home. But in truth, I had been sure so many times that I was wearying of certainty.

I beached the skiff and followed a narrow path through an alley of poplars; their tall elegance, like white spires reaching for the higher, lifted my spirits for the moment.

I had not walked far before I came upon the same fountain

with Neptune and his nymphs that I had seen earlier. Impaled on the sea god's trident, naked, with her arms hacked off above the elbows, was the young woman who had kissed my cheek and bade me goodbye. Her lover's head, minus his eyes, sat in the outstretched arms of a nymph, his torso draped over the fountain's rim. They were made of concrete.

I could not disgorge the horror, and to comfort myself took to telling them how happy I was for their love and how its flame had sparked in me a longing for life and even greater longing for my wife, whom I was now in despair of seeing again.

Despairing, too, of seeing ever again anything of my old life, which seemed a life of another world, one found in a book for children safe in their beds, in a cottage atop a hill dotted with sheep and ponies and little stars that come out at night to point you to sleep. Safe in a world that never existed, in a time that never was, I could hear my wife say, a world we dream of because ours is so frightening, as it always has been and always will be. My wife was always good for setting my course straight.

The children I had seen earlier, their band now swollen to fifty, reappeared in a silent, orderly file. Some held naked banners soaked in blood, some held aloft sheets festooned with ears and clumps of bloodied hair. Others flew kites streaming with strips of books and rags made from paintings. One teary-eyed boy crying for his mother fell behind. Three girls and a young man with a shaven head yanked him from the line and beat him with short oak clubs, drowning his face in clumps of blood and hair. Some of the marchers glanced my way as they passed by, but they paid me no attention, regarding me as neither friend nor foe but as I, in fact, was, an ineffectual man in a burning world.

I now took a path I seemed to remember when I first entered the park. The ground was strewn with branches of fallen jasmine bursting with sweetness where earlier it was carpeted with bitter green needles fallen from the pine trees. I was on a sweet path to where? I wondered. But I did not wonder long before I saw my wife in a hollow at the end of the wood. She was sitting there on a red blanket, a picnic basket bursting with wine bottles and blood sausages, and the young-old man, who had now become a youth, was lying by her side.

His smooth, tan face was at once young like the first dawn at sea and very old like unpolished marble from an ancient quarry. His was an ugly beauty, only elements of which, but never the whole, were ever before seen. His uniform was neither gray nor green, neither brown nor black, but all those colors blended into one color to which I could give no name and which did not before exist. I was sure of that, as I was sure of his great power born from a soil without flowers or sun but from some whole new earth that recognized neither. He flashed her a wide smile.

And she returned the smile—a flower not yet convinced it wanted to bloom—and took his hand. How much younger she seemed than when we kissed in our hotel room in the morning. Indeed, this was a park of rejuvenations. Except for myself, who followed old grooves of mind and fidelities, so useless now in this dynamic landscape where poets and lovers were murdered and ruthless children and their impassioned elders ruled.

Then he whispered some words in her ear and she smiled again—but this time the smile fully ripened and opened—and she brushed his cheek with her lips and sighed, as one would in presence of a god. Suddenly, as if by some switch, his face broke into discrete planes of shadows and light, of good and evil. In another instant, the planes cohered into one uniform surface transcending all categories of human value and known history.

He saw me first, reaching for his pistol as he took me in. In a flash, she followed his glance and, without a word, looked at me reproachfully, as if to say, What did you expect—keeping me waiting all this time? Is one to wait forever?

I have made a long journey, I wanted to answer, and have met with temptations and remained faithful despite them, but I could not speak, so amazed and pained was I to see her with another man, and one so young and so certain of his strength. He waved me away with his pistol, his expression at once indifferent and fierce, as if he had recognized before him a large, powerless boy of confused intentions. She was annoyed by my presence, her eyes said, with my interference in their pleasure. She made an impatient toss of her head, as if to say, *Leave*.

I slowly retreated, thinking there was time to sort all this out later, at the hotel, where I was bound to find her restored to our room and perhaps even to me, once the world was back in its usual, settled place. Then I thought I could not wait for that outcome, should it ever arrive. I imagined finding a thick stick in the brush and returning to the love nest and clubbing my rival's head at the height of his triumph. I cared less that he would shoot me than that, with his youth and strength, he would quickly overpower and humiliate me before my wife's eyes, leaving me in yet greater defeat and shame.

I was heavy with the black weight of loss. Isn't it enough that the world is tumbling down? I thought. Must my own little world go crashing down along with it? There is nothing so terrible in the world that makes one cry out more for justice than one's own hurt feelings. What is the suffering of the world compared to the pain of my toothache?

When I was a boy, I had a dog named Louis. A black Labrador with a limp, who would sit beside me at the dinner table and everywhere I sat. If he left my sight for a moment I went to search for him, and when I found him I put my arms about his neck and kissed him.

"Don't be a selfish boy," my mother said, when, for days, I bothered the house with my tears after finding Louis, poisoned by a neighbor, under the summer porch. Be considerate of us, she said, we who have to bear your unhappiness as if you were the only sad person in the world. Don't be selfish now, I told myself, thinking only of your wife's infidelity: consider the wider sadness of the world and not just your own plot. It was good advice, if only I could forgo my sense of falling from the sky long enough to heed it.

I took a new path filled with a twilight glow filtering through the trees. Soon I would be walking in darkness, in a park of roving wolves with scissor teeth. But strangely I was not afraid of the darkness, of the wolves, of the breeze of knives slicing through the trees, surrendering myself to the idea that all directions would inevitably lead me to other crimes, other shames in which I would have my part. But other hopes, too, I thought, other hopes.

I turned in the direction of a distant roar, until I found myself on an immense cliff, from whose height I could see great distances. Beneath me was spread all of the burning city, and in the far reaches I could see, as if they had been scaled to miniature, all the burning cities of the world, after which my view blended into an horizon of pulverized bricks, twisted steel, glowing embers, and dead dust.

Everywhere, above all the cities near and far, antique planes are circling. Everywhere bombs are bursting into handcuffs of flame. Everywhere lovers are roasting in burning beds, sheets fluttering like drunken sails. Everywhere poets are secreting books in caves and dry wells. Everywhere lovers are grasping for dreams jumping through burning windows. Everywhere poets are guiding poets through valleys of burn-ing rhymes. Everywhere museums are burning, paintings surrendering their images to smoke and fire. Everywhere dic-tionaries are forgetting their words page by page. Everywhere libraries are burning, books streaming ink from their gutters. Everywhere everything we had ever learned was burning, everywhere everything we had remembered or would remember was burning, everywhere everything we were and had dreamed of becoming was burning.

I stood with my back against the forest, stood there on a giant cliff, years above the spreading fires and the dying rubble below, my eyes searching everywhere for dawn.

The Ship at Anchor

Mother was old now. After all the years of being her son, I could finally judge her age: old. I wanted to say, Just yesterday you were still young, Mom, but today you're old. But that is not the thing you say to a mother, especially when she's come to visit and is settled by you on a porch in a wicker chair.

The boy was drawing, the sun was sliding into the pocket of the horizon; the ship lay tethered to a roving sea.

"The sea is roving under our eyes," my mother said.

"The sea is roving, Dad," the boy repeated. He was fond of replaying certain words when their sounds suggested a shape or an image to him. He often made drawings of sounds, like the word "sound" itself, which looked like an empty cave with a hanging lightbulb, or the word "pirate," which he once represented—in his more literal, realist period—as a rat-shaped pie with an eye patch and a needle-thin sword.

That was just a visual pun, I explained, a translation of parts of a word to a picture, and thus was much less interesting than his usual, more abstract and evocative images. He agreed, he said, but it was much harder to make images representing the heart of a word. Those images were painful to make, he said, because they did not come from his eyes but from a place deep inside him, from a place he had no words to describe.

From your soul, I wanted to say, but explaining that would have taken him too soon to a world he would one day, and on his own, discover. For now, he was drawing from life the ship at anchor in a flat sea. He put a full red moon above her bow, though there was none there in the sky, nothing glowing there at all, not even a hint of a star as the night fell. Soon we would have to put on the porch lights and soon we would have to go into the house.

"This will be for you, Nana," he said, holding up the unfinished drawing to his grandmother.

"Why don't I take you along with it?" she said. "Then I can have both of you all the time."

He laughed. "Nana, my Nana," he said.

"Do you want me to get you some tea?" I asked the mother.

"I'll be going home soon," she answered. "Stay here with me a while longer and let's devour the time together."

"Let's devour the whole night," I said. "Anyway, what's the point of going home when you're already home?" I liked her, my mother. I loved her as much as I had my wife.

The boy looked up from his drawing and said, "Don't go, Nana."

"I'll think about that," she said. "Come up here and give me a big hug first."

He rushed to her, throwing his arms about her neck.

"Stay with us, please," he said.

"Well, since you ask me so nicely, my dear boy," she said, "I think maybe I will."

"Stay forever," he said.

"Forever's a long time, don't you think?"

"Not long enough, Nana."

"Forever's an eternity. I'd gladly spend an eternity with you, just as we are, right now," she said, hugging him to her.

It was soon his bedtime. He made no fuss but asked that his grandmother come up and read to him, as she always did when she stayed with us.

Of course she would, she said, since little else in the world made her happier than to read to him, to be with him, to kiss those cheeks so smooth with childhood, and his eyes, she said, to kiss those eyes so sweet with life. She took his hand, letting him lead her, step by step, up the stairs to his blue room papered with stars.

When they left, I brought out my binoculars and took a

long look at the ship in the last light. She was a shabby hulk, black paint scaling off the bow, rigging flopping in the breeze, lines lying about uncoiled in slack heaps. Some men appeared now and then, smoking in a shiftless way, looking over the gunwales toward the shore, toward me, a speck on a porch. I waved, but no one answered.

The ship had lain there all day and into dusk and now, at night, lolled about with her running lights in dull glow, like a string of dirty pearls. When I went up to see the boy, the ship was out there, and even after I kissed him good night and turned off the light she was still there.

He was reading one of his *Tintin* books when I came in, looking up at me the last possible moment before he felt it impolite not to do so. He had good manners, in any case. You carry your civilization with you; his Nana had taught him that at an age when it could stick. He took to the idea instantly, seeing it as part of a game, which indeed it is. That was what had made him seem older than his years—his manners, and the kindness beneath them, which gave them value.

"I'm sorry," I said. "I know you want to go on reading but it's time for sleep."

"Well," he said, as if considering the point, "why don't *you* read to me?"

"It would be the same thing," I said, "because you would still be up and awake."

He nodded. He seldom argued unless he thought I or the world was being unfair. "Unjust" being his ultimate word of disapproval. A friend who had struck him in the back or a teacher who berated him for another's wrongdoing was unjust, as was the world that caused night to come before its time. Tintin was his hero, because he was a boy who sought justice and fought to set the world right in all places and at all times of day.

"What does that ship want out there, Dad?" he asked.

"Who knows? Nothing much; it's just floating about until something better comes along." The odd truth was that she didn't drift much the whole day, her position staying fixed as the sea itself dragged at her anchor and the wind pulled her from stem to stern, roving her about.

"You know," he said, "there's a ship just like that in *Tintin*, where the sailors keep the captain drunk so they can do whatever they want."

"What did they want, my son?"

"To do mischief, Dad."

"You must know a lot about that stuff," I said.

"Not me, Dad. I just do good mischief."

"The mischief is that you just tricked me into letting you stay awake three more minutes."

He laughed, having seen the justice in that.

"Good night, then, Dad." He waited for me to kiss him. The final one until morning and the protective seal against the bumps in the night.

I turned out the light and left the door open a fist wide so he'd see the reassuring hall light if he woke up in the dark. I stood by the door a few moments until I was certain he was asleep and safe in his dreams. Then I made another visit.

Mother was in her room reading. Ever since I could remember, she read in bed before going to sleep. One of her few certainties, everything else just slips away, she always said. As her husband did—in good health, in good mood. In love with his wife, with his work, with his son, me.

In a second he was gone. Midsentence, so to speak. On the phone laughing with an old friend one minute and in the mute other world the next, the phone still in his hand. Comical, actually. As if Death had no interest in hearing the whole conversation. What is so pressing that makes Death so curt, so interruptive of the narrative? Death, clearly, has no sense or desire for the complete story, which means he has no curiosity. Which is why he is so flat, so empty. A silhouette of action.

"Reading again, Mom? After lights-out!"

"Oh! Just catching up with the past," she said. She had earlier gone down to my library and pulled out Bunyan's *The Pilgrim's Progress*.

"A heavy stone before sleep, don't you think, Mom?"

"Not heavy enough," she said. "I was looking for *The Magic Mountain*, but you seem to be all out."

"I'll have it for next time," I said, "and in German."

"Does he miss her very much?" she asked abruptly.

"He doesn't say. But until a little while ago he used to call out for her in his sleep."

"You know that I generally love you," she said, turning from her book, "but I love him more."

"Maybe you just love him more freshly. In any case, I'd feel the same."

"I'd like to be around a while longer, long enough to see him when he first falls in love. That would be sweet," she said.

"He's always in love now," I said. "Every week a new fling."

"Not that way," she said. "The passionate way, I mean."

She was once a beautiful woman, my mother; she was a handsome one now, more vain of her figure than when she was young, when she said that only the mind mattered, that while the body grew old and ugly, the mind lasted in its attractiveness. Mothers always tell their sons that, hoping they will not be stupid when they grow up, hoping they will not mistake the beautiful form for the soul in it, although sometimes the two may be joined.

"You mean the sexual way, Mom. Isn't that what you mean?"

"That, too, of course. But mostly I want to be there to help mend his broken heart the first time it gets broken."

"Anyway," I said, mouthing the platitude one says to the old, "you still have a long time ahead of you." She gave me a sly look: Who's kidding whom? it said.

"Let me have ten more years, until he's seventeen. He'll be fully ripe then for love."

"And what about you, Mom? Are you ripe for another love?"

"Not just now," she said. "Right now I'm just roving. I'd rather meet a new book than a new man."

"I thought you had read them all," I said.

"Just the good ones," she said.

I took her hand and kissed it. "You'll outlive us all, Mom," I said.

"I'd rather not," she said. "I'd just be left alone with bad books in bad bindings."

I kissed her hand again, longer this time. And then once again. It was an old hand, like the parchment of a pirate map. "Sweet dreams," I said. "Till morning," I said. Exactly her words to me at bedtime when I was my son's age. She'd blow me a kiss, and I'd imagine the cloud of her breath coating me with an invisible armor against all the world's harm.

"I may make an early start," she said. "I may be gone before you wake."

I shrugged and turned up my palms as if to say, As you wish. My protests would have been pointless. Not my son's, though: what is more persuasive, after all, than a child's earnest plea?

I went out and across the field to my studio. My mother's light was still on even some while after I started trying to work. Where was she now in Bunyan's pilgrimage, I wondered, and what was so compelling about it to keep her awake for so long? The world and its stories, we're famished for them, and maybe, I thought, that is why Death is so jealous of us, since he has no story and is just an agent of terminations.

I was not an exceptional painter. I had gotten used to that idea long ago, before the boy was born, before I met my wife and fell in love. It was good for us that I had made that accommodation with myself before we met or I would have been an unhappy husband and a miserable father, gnawing at myself for my limits. What I could do well, I did. I found pleasure in the work so long as I did not yearn for what I was incapable of becoming in my dreams—an artist who painted what had never before been seen and who thus made the world newer and more interesting. The boy might one day do that. He was, I liked to think, already on that path.

I excelled in paintings of seascapes and harbor scenes, boats in port at sunset—lighthouses on cliffs in the whirl of a white storm I also did very successfully. Not very original work, but mine, I liked to think; work which was rewarded not lavishly but sufficiently well enough to keep a decent life.

For my own pleasure, perhaps for the glow, the vanity of the association, I made copies of narrative paintings long disregarded by modernists but still beloved by a few, myself included, obviously. Poussin was then in progress on my easel. Not him, naturally, but his painting in which shepherds are contemplating a plinth inscribed with the words *Ego in Arcadia Sum*—"Even in Arcadia I am." Meaning Death is omnipresent, even in the most beautiful places, where life richly abounds, where bounty reigns. I had still to finish the figure of the shepherdess, a woman ravishingly solid and simple, like an Ionian temple in a sacred grove of cypresses. I had been stuck for a while trying to complete her, because each time I painted her face, it was not the face

Poussin had rendered but the young face of my dead wife. As if my mind saw one thing but my hand another, and nothing I did made the face look as I intended. I sometimes thought it a good thing, a sign of something original living within me. But, finally, I could not bring myself to let my little hint of romantic autobiography disfigure Poussin's masterpiece, so I sponged out my wife's face, leaving the shepherdess's torso headless, in white, anonymous space. Audacity in art and in life was never my style. Even at the end, when Death comes and pays his one and only visit, I know that I'll follow him meekly, acquiescent and compliant. No trouble, I'll say. Here I come.

I stayed in this self-defeating mood—the best to keep one from working—for who knows how long, when the boy rushed in barefoot, pale, and frightened.

"Did you have a bad dream?" I asked, lifting him up in my arms.

He had, and when he woke he went first to my room, where I was not, and then to his Nana's room, where she was sleeping in a strange way. When he tried to wake her she would not wake. And so he came to me.

She was still in her bed sleeping, her book open. She was sleeping with blank eyes fixed on words. Was the story that bad, Mom, I wanted to ask, that you would rather have died than continue reading it, calling for Death to spare you from another boring syllable?

Nana was sleeping a sleep of sorts, I told my son. The sleep that carries you to the edge of life and then drops you into another life, one which we could not join while still awake. That was what I told him.

She was now where his mother had gone, where we all one day would go, where our souls would go, his and mine, too. The soul, I said, thinking it was now the best time to tell him, was that strange, unknown, invisible thing he felt inside him when he made drawings of sounds.

He knew that, he said, he had known it for a long time because Nana had taught him that long ago. But all that didn't matter because he wanted his Nana here, with him, and not there with them.

"With whom do you mean?" I asked.

"With the men in the ship," he said. He had dreamt that she was taken there, and that was what had woken him, his dream of her being carried away to the ship. So he was glad when he saw that she was still there in bed, until he realized, when she would not wake, that it was the other, invisible part of her they had taken away.

"That was a sweet dream," I said, "but only a dream."

"It was not a dream," he said. She was there on that ship and, he added firmly, we should go there and rescue her.

"Tomorrow," I said, "in the morning," after he had a good night's sleep and thought things over in the daylight, in the light that dispelled dreams and brought them to reason.

"It'll be too late then, Dad," he said. "We'll never get her back if we wait." My boy looked so much older now, when he spoke, older than I was, older and more knowing than the sea when it lies flat and blue in its bed.

"I believe you, my dear boy," I said. "Yes, of course, we must go."

And off we went, down to the dinghy, the boy at the prow and me at the oars, and we rowed out to the ship, glowing cherry-red under the full red moon.

And no sooner had we reached the ship's black hull than we were wafted aloft by a magical wind to its disorderly deck and just as soon, as if on an elevator cloud, we floated below to a drab galley amidships and landed among a sullen, noisy crew and its unshaven, peg-legged captain—who got right down to business.

"You can't have her," he said.

"Then Death will," the boy said.

The crew went silent and looked about apprehensively. I was astonished at his words, almost as much as I was by all the events that had led to them. He seemed so certain, my boy, of things unknown and strange, and it was clear that he was strongly in charge of himself and that I was now under his wing.

Then the captain laughed and, emboldened by him, the others followed suit, but hollowly.

"What do you know about this matter, my little fellow?" he asked nervously.

"Enough to make you be sorry," my son said.

"Sit down," the captain said, "and let's palaver like gentlemen of the world."

He waved his arm and suddenly the grim galley glowed with rich furniture and golden lamps, and there appeared out of the air a huge candlelit table heaped with golden bowls of fruit and nuggets of chocolates wrapped in gold tissue. The captain beckoned my son to sit beside him, waving me to the table's other end, where I sat beside a man in silver trousers and a shirt so blue I could see the sky.

"Well, lad, what have you got to say?" the captain asked, spearing a red pear with a silver poniard.

"Well, sir, I want Nana's soul and I want it back inside her."

"I have her soul, but I can't undo what Death has done, and neither can you. So that's the final word on that," he said, slicing his pear to a sliver the weight of a breath. The crew murmured their approval of their captain's firmness.

"Hear, hear," my table mate called out.

"I understand, Captain," my boy said. "Death has his power and you have yours."

"Quite," the captain said.

"But you've stolen my Nana's soul from Death."

"Let's say we got it on its way to somewhere else. Right, my lads?"

I understood at last that we were on a pirate ship of souls. That these pirates had waylaid my mother's soul from its true journey through the world's seamless mystery.

"What do you do with the souls you've pirated?" I asked.

"We shred them for mulch," he said, with a big wink of the eye that was not patched.

"We trade them," my table companion said. "Small souls for larger, large souls for grand souls, grand souls for noble ones."

"Whom do you trade with?" my boy asked.

"Why with other pirates, of course," the blue shirt answered.

"Enough," the captain said. "We're not here for disquisitions."

"My Nana had a noble soul, I'm sure," the boy said.

"Of great value, of incredible value, of priceless value. What have you of trading value to match her worth?" the captain asked.

My son whispered into the captain's ear, whispered something that piqued the pirate chief to cough up a sigh of a thousand fish-eyed bubbles.

"Even if you could do that, why would I care?" the captain said when the last bubble burst into a little hand of flame.

"Because then you can always see him."

"See what?" the captain shouted.

"See him," my boy said.

"Well," the captain said, "this needs some thought." He called his men to gather around him, speaking to them so softly that I could not catch his words.

One of the pirates exclaimed, "Trumped by a boy!"

"Still," the captain said, turning to my son, "I don't see the usefulness in having the grim one's picture. It's not," he said in an aside to his crew, "that he's such a looker."

"But you may find a use one day," my son said, ignoring

the crew's roar of laughter. "Maybe you will trade with Death something you want."

"That's an idea, Captain," said the man with the blue shirt. "Maybe we can get him not to bother us so much, him always pestering us to give back the souls we've snatched."

"What would Death want to trade, my brave bucko? Nothing pleases him, nothing interests him, nothing satisfies him, except the taking from Life everything that lives."

"He may want," my boy said, in a voice firm enough to drive a nail through a beam, "not to be seen."

"Show me, boy," the captain said, "then we'll decide who gets what."

"But you must first promise to give back her soul to where it belongs."

"Oh! I promise," the captain said with a wink to his men.

My boy began drawing on a large white napkin, holding it up to the captain when he was finished.

"Doesn't look like much to me," the captain said, turning the napkin about this way and that.

"It's not his picture," I said, "it's a transcription of his name to his image. The boy can do that with most sounds. He can do that with your name, if you want."

"I have no name," the captain said, looking frightened. "So don't be asking me for one."

"None of us have names, neither," said the man in the blue shirt. "Isn't that right, men?"

"No, no, no," they said in a chorus. "None of us have any kind of names."

"Because when you say his name," I continued, "the sound of it vanishes into the air and he vanishes along with it, keeping all his power with him."

The captain remained silent for a moment, then beckoned his men to gather about him in a circle, where they spoke in crowish barks, very sharp and unsettling. I was fearful and thought of quietly taking my son back to our dinghy and over the dark water, back to our house, where we would be safe.

"Let's go, my boy," I whispered. "Let's leave while there's still time."

"No, Dad," he said firmly. "You go, if you want. I need to stay."

I was so amazed by his audacity that I almost forgot that he was just a boy and that I was his father and with a father's authority. But just as I was about to assert myself, the captain broke from his men, returning to us, his arms crossed, his face a powdery white smoke.

"We have decided to keep your drawing and to keep your grandmother's soul, to boot. What do you say to that?"

"That Death has many names in many languages, and that now you have his image in only one of them. You can steal my picture but you still won't have the drawings of his other names, drawings that I could trade with you when you needed me to."

"A valiant answer from such a small boy. But then, even for

a brave boy you are brave," the captain said, giving me a look I took to mean that in the area of courage the son surpassed the father.

The blue-shirted man came up and whispered into the captain's ear, a long whisper, the length of a woolen string. The captain nodded slowly and turned to me and my son.

"Let's go above deck," he said.

Before I could say a word, we were all above deck, under a black heaven, moonless and distraught. I put my arm about my son's waist and held him fast.

"You've won, my boy," the captain said. "Your grandmother's soul is going where it belongs."

"Let me see it," my son said.

"You can't see it," the blue-shirted man said. "It has no visibility."

"Nor weight, nor color, nor odor," the captain added. "It has nothing of the qualities you expect in your world."

"How will I know you've freed her soul, then," my boy asked, "how will I know you've kept your word?"

"Stand very still," the captain ordered. "And you right beside him," he said, pointing to me with his sword. "Notice that there is no wind, no breeze, no movement of air, that there is only stillness and the flat screen of night."

"Yes," I said, "there's not the faintest stir."

"Now hold your breath, the two of you."

We stayed very still, not breathing, and suddenly felt, for the quickest of seconds, a feathery whisper brush our faces.

"That's that, then," the captain said.

"That's what?" I asked, annoyed by his mumbo jumbo, by what I thought were his theatrical airs.

"Her last breath just flew by you," he said, "her last breath, carrying her soul."

At his final words, we found ourselves, my boy and I, returned to our house. The ship had vanished, leaving, where it had once been, a black line of sea.

I carried my sleepy son to his bed and left his sleeping self to digest the night. I went to my room, thinking I would read and reflect on the night's strange and wonderful events, and then, at early morning, I would start my mother's procession—my wife's same route—from house to funeral parlor, and from there to the grave. I always kept a stack of books on the night table, books I chose randomly and whose pages I read in no order and in small bites. For this reason I read little fiction, enjoying poetry and aphoristic writings, by artists, especially. It was to Ingres I turned to that night, thinking to find a sweet passage to ease me from images of death and pirated souls. "A true line," it read, "is closer to god than any church." It was a noble thought, designed to assure artists of their value, or to make them feel inadequate and forever striving.

I repeated the sentence a few times and then shut my eyes for the next few hours before daylight. Somehow, the artist's words made me more melancholy than the fantastic events on the pirate ship, more sad than my mother's death, which already seemed so long ago, before there were mothers. Those words made me wonder why I ever wanted to be an artist, why I ever wanted to live, though I never thought I wanted to die. I tried very hard to quiet myself, to calm my thoughts, but I could not.

I wondered how my son was faring after such a powerful night, so I went down to his room but he was not in his bed, which was perfectly made, as if the housekeeper had come and trimmed the sheets and flattened out the blankets. I went from room to room, went up to the attic and down to the basement, searching and searching for my boy. I went to my mother's room, but he was not there, either, or, oddly enough, was she. I would think about her later; for the moment, however, I was not concerned about the mother, knowing that wherever her body was mattered little, now that her soul was on its adventures. I had not yet started to grieve her death, so busy was I in the events of the night, but I knew that I had an eternity before me to grieve.

I went out to my studio, sure that my son had gone there, where he had often come with his mother to visit me at my work, where he felt safe among the stacks of drawings and tubes of paint, safe in the place where, for all my regrets of not being the artist I had dreamed of being, I had been most happy. He liked my happiness, my boy, as had his mother; it made them feel safe, where nothing much else was safe.

Imagine, I started to say, imagine that my mother had so little control over life as to have her husband die on the phone in midsentence and imagine how she had so little to say over things that she herself had died in midread, so to speak. So little control over our life and none in death and its aftermath, no voice to say where your soul went, if it went anywhere at all, granted it had not been plucked from your last breath and stowed aboard a pirate ship for trading.

"Don't give it a thought," my mother answered, once, when as boy I asked where we went when we died. I did not give it a thought for a long time, having erased the question from my view until after my wife died. But soon after, I wondered whether the dead ever missed the living, or whether they entered a new world where nothing of the past lived and where no one who had lived in it any longer mattered. My mother dreamed of an eternity spent in a library, where she could read all the books of the world in all their languages. How many millions of books there would be, Mom, I said, awed by such a vast project. Yes, she said, but one day, in just another day of eternity, she would have read every book ever written, and then where would she be?

The studio—except for the feeling of stale dust and emptiness—was much as I had left it except that the paintings looked tired, sagging on their stretchers. Paintings need to be seen or they languish, wither, and die on the vine. My unfinished Poussin was leaning—languishing—against a windowless wall, though I was sure I had left it on the easel when I went out to visit the ship at anchor. I would have loved to have finished that canvas, and this time I hoped I would have the courage to paint my wife's face where the shepherdess's was supposed to be. The courage to leave, for however long it lasted, a trace of my heart.

My son was not in the studio, even though the morning sunlight now flooded the large sad room. What I mean is that, although it was light, he had still not appeared. Whatever that meant, I was worried now, because I missed him so much, and I was frightened of a life where I would always miss him.

"I miss you, too, of course," I said guiltily to my wife, in case she had read my thoughts from somewhere in the universe. "And I will miss you, as well," I said to my mother, not wanting her to feel left unloved. But, of course, missing a son is different from missing all others, who return to you in various guises. But unlike the swallows, sons do not return in the spring.

In the middle of my musings, the door opened and my son came in with a beautiful young woman. He was tall now, with a faint red mustache, and he walked with a seaman's gait, as if to steady himself against the rolling deck of the world. He had his arm about the beautiful woman's waist. She was full of smiles for him and he held her like a man confident he is loved. I was happy for him and wished my mother could see him, a young man in love.

"Dad," he said with a sigh, a low sigh of evocation, memory, and longing. Then he slowly looked about the studio, even above, at the beams under the high open ceiling, looked about as if searching for me and our old life there. But I was nowhere to be found.

Dedications

"Voyagers." For Walter Mosley.

"Self Portrait with Sicily." For Karen Marta.

"Self Portrait with Bullfight." For Iris Smyles.

"Self Portrait with Circus." For Richard Howard.

"The Park Near Marienbad." For Francine du Plessix Gray.

"Self Portrait with Cheese." For Roy and the Three Bears.

"Self Portrait with Icebergs." For Pierre Huyghe and Francesca Grassi.

"Self Portrait with Beach." For Mona Kuhn.

"The Park in Winter." For Dorothy Lichtenstein.

"The Bar on Tompkins Square Park:
Self Portrait with Blue Horse." For Eric Fischl.

"The Park on Fire." Homage to Federico García Lorca.

"The Ship at Anchor." For Kenji Coleman Yamada.

Acknowledgments

I want to thank: Jill Bialosky, my editor, for her loyalty and for seeing that these stories have their twice-told life; Gloria Loomis, my agent, for her measureless support and her friendship; Dorothy Lichtenstein, under whose affectionate sky many of these stories were written; Bradford Morrow, who started me again on the road of short fictions; Hans Ulrich Obrist and his marriages of art and literature; Iris Smyles for her invaluable reading of these stories; David Lichtenstein for his steadfast encouragement. My gratitude and love to Karen Marta for her care in seeing me and this book through.

These stories appeared previously in the following publications:

"Prologue." *Writers on Writing*, Volume II, Times Books. New York: Henry Holt, 2004.

"Voyagers." In "An Anatomy of Roads," ed. Bradford Morrow, *Conjunctions* 44, Spring 2005.

"Self Portrait with Sicily." *Conjunctions* 50, Spring 2008.

"Self Portrait with a Bullfight." A bilingual edition with an introductory essay by María Lozano. Publicaciones de la Residencia de Estudiantes; Madrid, May 2010.

"The Park Near Marienbad." In "Cinema Lingua," ed. Bradford Morrow, *Conjunctions* 42, Spring 2004.

"Self Portrait with Cheese." Roy Lichtenstein: *Conversations with Surrealism*, exhibition catalogue: Mitchell-Innes & Nash. October 2005. Reprinted in *Smyles & Fish*, vol. 1, Fall 2006.

"Self Portrait with Icebergs." Pierre Huyghe *Celebration Park* catalogue for the Pierre Huyghe exhibition at the Musée d'art moderne de la Ville de Paris, February 2006. Reprinted in *KGBBarLit*, Fall 2007.

"Self Portrait with Beach." Mona Kuhn *Evidence* catalogue for show in New York City, 2007. Reprinted in *Conjunctions* 48, in "Faces of Desire," ed. Bradford Morrow, Spring 2007. Reprinted in *Harper's*, August 2007.

"The Park in Winter." *Fence* 8, nos. 1 and 2, Summer 2005.

"The Bar on Tompkins Square Park: Self Portrait with Blue Horse." *BOMB*, Summer 2009. Podcast on BOMBsite, June 25, 2009.

"The Park on Fire." In the catalogue *Everstill/Siempretodavía*, Fundación Federico García Lorca and Sociedad Estatal de Conmemoraciones Culturales (SECC), Ministerio de Cultura, Gobierno de España, December 2010.

"The Ship at Anchor." In "Wish You Were Here," ed. Ian Jack, *Granta* 91.

About the Author

Frederic Tuten grew up in the Bronx in the wake of the Great Depression. At age fifteen, he dropped out of high school to become a painter and live in Paris, but that youthful dream went unrealized. He took odd jobs and studied briefly at the Art Students League, and eventually went back to school, continuing on to earn a PhD in early nineteenth-century American literature from New York University.

He later traveled through Latin and South America, studied pre-Columbian and Mexican mural painting at the University of Mexico, wrote about Brazilian Cinema Novo, and joined that circle of filmmakers that included Glauber Rocha and Nelson Pereira dos Santos. Tuten finally did live in Paris, where he taught film and literature at the University of Paris 8. He acted in a short film by Alain Resnais, cowrote the cult film *Possession*, and conducted summer writing workshops with Paul Bowles in Tangiers.

Tuten's short stories and art and film criticism have appeared in such places as *ArtForum*, the *New York Times*, *Vogue*, *Conjunctions*, *Granta*, and *Harper's*. In addition, he has written essays and fiction for artists' catalogues, including John Baldessari, Eric Fischl, Pierre Huyghe, Jeff Koons, David Salle, and Roy Lichtenstein. He has published five novels: *The*

Adventures of Mao on the Long March, Tallien: A Brief Romance, Tintin in the New World, Van Gogh's Bad Café, and *The Green Hour.*

Tuten received a Guggenheim Fellowship for Fiction and was given the Award for Distinguished Writing from the American Academy of Arts and Letters.